"I can't stand the thought of my daughter being afraid of me," Caleb whispered.

"She's not," Noelle whispered back. "After all, she let you hold her in the pool, remember?"

He shook his head. "She wanted to swim so badly I think she would have let anyone hold her."

Noelle sank down into the chair next to him, unable to refute his logic. "She needs a little time, that's all."

He lifted his gaze to hers. "Maybe I can find a safe place for the two of you to stay for a while. Then I'll head off on my own to try and figure out who's trying to kill me."

For some odd reason, Noelle found she was beginning to believe Caleb was in fact innocent of the crime he'd been accused of.

But knowing that didn't reassure her the way she thought it would.

Because whoever had tried to kill Caleb outside her house was very likely still looking for him. And she was deeply afraid that the killer wouldn't hesitate to take the life of a woman and child, too, if necessary.

Books by Laura Scott

Love Inspired Suspense

The Thanksgiving Target
Secret Agent Father
The Christmas Rescue
Lawman-in-Charge
Proof of Life
Identity Crisis
Twin Peril
Undercover Cowboy
Her Mistletoe Protector
*Wrongly Accused

*SWAT: Top Cops

LAURA SCOTT

grew up reading faith-based romance books by Grace Livingston Hill, but as much as she loved the stories, she longed for a bit more mystery and suspense. She is honored to write for the Love Inspired Suspense line, where a reader can find a heartwarming journey of faith amid the thrilling danger.

Laura lives with her husband of twenty-five years and has two children, a daughter and a son, who are both in college. She works as a critical-care nurse during the day at a large level-one trauma center in Milwaukee, Wisconsin, and spends her spare time writing romance.

Please visit Laura at www.laurascottbooks.com, as she loves to hear from her readers.

WRONGLY ACCUSED

LAURA SCOTT

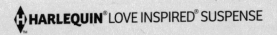

HARLEQUIN® LOVE INSPIRED® SUSPENSE

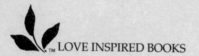 LOVE INSPIRED BOOKS

ISBN-13: 978-0-373-44591-2

WRONGLY ACCUSED

For I, the Lord, love justice; I hate robbery and wrongdoing. In my faithfulness I will reward my people and make an everlasting covenant with them.
—*Isaiah* 61:8

This book is dedicated to Pat and Ted Iding.
Thank you for all the wonderful years you've loved me
as one of your own.

ONE

Caleb O'Malley's stomach knotted painfully at the thought of seeing his daughter, Kaitlin, for the first time in over a year. Since the day he'd been sent to jail for a crime he didn't commit.

He parked his beat-up truck in front of the fourth house from the corner and killed the engine. Taking a deep breath, he shoved his car door open and forced himself to get out and walk up the sidewalk to the front door of Noelle Whitman's house, trying not to resent the woman who'd been his daughter's foster mother while he'd been behind bars.

To be honest, it was his own fault he hadn't seen Kaitlin in so long. At first, he'd thought he'd be let out as soon as they realized he was innocent. But then week after week passed by, and he'd grimly realized there was a very real possibility he'd be found guilty. At that point, he'd been unable to bear the thought of having his young daughter see him in jail.

He'd been shocked to hear from his lawyer that the case against him had been dropped due to the strange disappearance of the eyewitness. And deeply glad to know he was free at last.

He rapped sharply on the door and waited impatiently for the Whitman woman to answer.

He squinted against the harsh glare of the summer sun. After not being in the sunlight for so long, he enjoyed the warmth soaking into his skin, even though the temperature was hovering at a steamy ninety degrees.

His lawyer, Jack Owens, had promised to let Ms. Whitman know Caleb was on his way to pick up Kaitlin, so there was no reason for her not to be here. Hard to believe that he'd only been out of jail for a few hours. His release had been so sudden he hadn't had time to make plans. It was Friday and once he picked up Kaitlin, he'd go home and take the weekend to figure out how to start their life over again.

He lifted his hand to knock again at the exact moment the door swung open, so he pulled back his hand just in time. The woman standing before him was much younger than he'd anticipated, probably barely thirty, with reddish-gold hair and fair skin. She was dressed casually in a green short-sleeved sweater and calf-length blue jeans. In her arms was his five-year-old daughter, wearing a pretty pink dress and pink barrettes clipped to her glossy chin-length blond hair. She clutched a small stuffed giraffe to her chest.

The minute Kaitlin saw him she dropped the giraffe, wrapped her arms around Noelle's neck and burst into tears. "Nooo, I don't wanna go wif Daddy!"

His stomach tightened painfully as his worst nightmare played out in front of him. Ms. Whitman held Kaitlin close at the same time she took a step back, a wary expression on her face.

"You'd better come in," she said over Kaitlin's sobs. He stepped forward and bent down to pick up the giraffe.

A split second later, he heard the crack of a rifle and

the soft thud of a bullet hitting the doorframe of the house, inches from where his head had been.

"Get back," he shouted, barging into her house with the finesse and strength of a bull, before slamming the door behind him.

Another bullet pierced the door, followed by yet another. He covered Noelle's body with his as he practically pushed her toward the relative safety of the kitchen.

"What's going on?" Noelle asked hoarsely, her green eyes wide with fear as he shoved her down behind the island. He hated the way Kaitlin's crying grew louder.

"We have to get out of here." There wasn't time to explain what he didn't even understand himself. He had no clue why someone was shooting at him, but right now all that mattered was getting out of here in one piece. He lunged for the keys he saw lying on the counter and mentally visualized where the garage was located. "Does that door lead out to the garage?"

"Yes."

"Let's go."

"No! Wait! We have to call 911!" She shrank away from him, pressing herself against the island and curling protectively around his daughter.

He hesitated, trying to think rationally. He didn't trust the police, but if he left on his own would the shooter follow him and leave Ms. Whitman and Kaitlin alone?

Or use his daughter as bait as a way to draw him out? The very possibility made his blood run cold.

"Look, we need to get out of here. There's a chance that guy out there will try to use Kaitlin as a way to get to me. I have to keep her safe!"

The sound of breaking glass made him glance back toward the living room. A familiar round canister landed and rolled on the carpet with smoke rising up toward the ceiling.

"Tear gas! Listen, lady, if you want to live, come with me. I promise to keep you and Kaitlin safe. But we have to move. Now!" His eyes were already starting to burn as he grabbed the pink backpack that was on the counter next to the keys, gripped her arm and dragged her toward the door to the garage. "Hurry!"

Thankfully she followed him into the fresh air of the garage. She slid into the backseat and talked softly to Kaitlin as she buckled his daughter into her booster seat. He tossed the pink backpack inside and climbed into the driver's seat.

"Buckle up," he said tersely as he cranked the key in the ignition. The moment he heard her seat belt click he put the SUV in gear. Thankfully she drove a sturdy vehicle, which would help them escape the shooter. The thought of backing out the driveway in full view of the shooter filled him with dread. But he mentally visualized the neighborhood, marking a path that should help keep them safe.

"Hang on," he warned before he hit the garage door opener. As the door slowly opened he decided not to wait for it to get all the way up before he stomped hard on the accelerator and flew out of the driveway, clipping the bottom of the garage door with the top of her car.

The sound of gunfire filled the air as he swiftly spun the SUV around and headed straight across the street through a neighbor's yard.

Noelle let out a small scream as he barreled out of the garage, wrecking her garage door as he sailed down the driveway. At the sound of gunfire, she leaned over, trying to protect Kaitlin as Caleb O'Malley drove like a maniac across the street and through her neighbor's yard. She momentarily closed her eyes and frantically prayed.

Dear Lord, please keep me and Kaitlin safe!

The vehicle jerked sharply from side to side as they went up and over the edge of her neighbor's flower bed. Within moments, they were heading down that neighbor's driveway to the street behind hers.

Kaitlin's father didn't speak as he drove, taking several sharp turns as he took them farther away from her house. The way he kept glancing at the rearview mirror told her he was worried they were being followed.

Should she mention how she'd noticed a black pickup truck following behind her for the past few days? Was it possible that person had just been waiting for Kaitlin's father to show up?

She swiped at her eyes and glanced back, wishing desperately there was a cop somewhere close by. Where were the police when you needed them? Hopefully one of her neighbors had heard the gunshots and called the cops. If only she hadn't left her cell phone and her purse in her bedroom. But how was she to have known something like this would happen?

She pulled herself together with an effort. She could not let this man know how afraid she really was.

Kaitlin finally stopped crying, but her thumb was planted firmly in her mouth, a sure sign that the child was upset.

When Kaitlin's father headed toward the freeway, she forced herself to speak. "Why aren't we going to the closest police station?"

"Because I don't trust the police."

Her stomach knotted further and she had to work to keep her tone steady. "Where are you taking us?"

"Somewhere safe," he said, barely glancing back at her.

Somewhere safe? She swallowed a hysterical laugh. Everyone in Milwaukee knew he'd been arrested for killing his wife fourteen months ago. Caleb O'Malley had made headline news, not just in the city but across the country. *Former sharpshooter for the Milwaukee County Sheriff's Department SWAT team arrested for murdering his wife.*

Unfortunately, all charges against Caleb O'Malley had been dropped when the eyewitness, who claimed to have seen O'Malley shoot his wife and then take off from the scene of the crime, abruptly disappeared a week before the trial. Without the witness there wasn't enough of a case against him. At least that was what his lawyer, Jack Owens, had told her.

Noelle had been sick at the thought of handing Kaitlin back over to her father, but there hadn't been much she could do to prevent him from exercising his custodial right to take his daughter. Supposedly he wasn't a criminal anymore.

Still, she knew there was no statute of limitations for murder. There was a part of her that believed the police would eventually find the evidence they needed to lock up Caleb O'Malley for good. If he was guilty, of course, which she was fairly certain he was.

Had she gone with one killer to escape another?

"Why don't you let me and Kaitlin go?" she said, striving to sound reasonable. "Surely you don't want to expose your daughter to danger."

He concentrated on the road. "I told you, I can't ignore the possibility they would use her to get to me. I thought about dropping you off somewhere, but obviously Kaitlin needs you so that's not an option. I promise I'm not going to hurt you."

He was right about one thing: Kaitlin did need her.

No way was she leaving the child alone with a potential murderer. Yet she knew she was risking her life by staying. Granted, he'd tried to protect her back at the house when the bullets had started flying, but what did she really know about this man? Nothing except what she learned through the media.

And none of that had been good.

Trusting men wasn't exactly easy for her, either.

"Did you see anything out on the street?" he asked, breaking into her thoughts.

"You mean before the gunshots?" She thought back to those moments when she'd faced Caleb O'Malley across the threshold. Ironically, there hadn't been the usual black car she'd noticed over the past few days. "There was a red pickup parked on the street."

"That's my truck. Did you see anything else? Another vehicle? A person? Anything?"

"No." She'd been far more preoccupied with trying to find a way to ease the transition for Kaitlin. Noelle had planned to invite him in, hoping he'd spend some time getting to know his daughter again before leaving with her. Especially after the way Kaitlin had clung to her, sobbing.

As much as she feared the dark-haired stranger, she wasn't leaving Kaitlin alone with him any time soon. Kaitlin was the sole reason she'd come along in the first place. The poor child had already been through so much, losing her mother and then her father. Kaitlin had suffered night terrors the first weeks she'd been with Noelle, but the child hadn't had a nightmare for almost five months.

Noelle would be shocked if today's events didn't bring them back. She'd be surprised if her own nightmares of the past didn't return, too.

There was another long silence and she realized they were already well outside the city limits. Grimly she knew they could go for several hundred miles without stopping on the gas tank she'd filled yesterday.

"I'd let you both go if I could," he said in a low voice. "But I'm afraid it's too late. You and Kaitlin are in danger now, too."

"In danger from whom?" she asked helplessly.

"I wish I knew," he said, his tone weary. "Probably from the same person who killed Heather."

She knew Heather had been his wife and Kaitlin's mother. And if he thought she was going to believe that line of baloney, he was as crazy as the media had portrayed him to be.

During an interview on TV, one of his SWAT teammates had mentioned Caleb's hair-trigger temper. She could imagine how difficult it must have been for him to discover his wife was cheating on him.

Not that his wife had deserved to die for her sins, leaving Kaitlin without a mother, or a father once Caleb had been arrested. As Kaitlin's preschool teacher and an approved foster parent, she'd fought for and won temporary custody of the little girl. At first she thought it would only be a few weeks until other family had been notified but no one had been found. Over the past year she'd grown to love Kaitlin. And being forced to turn the child over to Caleb had nearly broken her heart.

"I guess you don't believe in the theory of innocent until proven guilty," he said, breaking into her thoughts.

"I never said you were guilty," she said hastily. No sense in baiting the tiger. She needed to keep on his good side in order to convince him to let her and Kaitlin go. So far, she wasn't entirely sure she believed in his theory that she and Kaitlin were in danger.

"So you believe I'm innocent?" he asked after several long moments.

She licked her dry lips and tried to smile. "The judge let you go, which is good enough for me."

He let out a noise that sounded suspiciously like a snort, but didn't say anything more. She stared out the window as the miles zipped past. Glancing over at Kaitlin, she noted the girl's eyelids were starting to droop. Long car rides tended to make the little girl sleepy and no doubt she'd worn herself out with her crying jag.

Twenty minutes later, Noelle realized Kaitlin's father had left the freeway and turned onto a country highway.

She couldn't quell a hint of panic when she didn't recognize the area. They were in a rural part of Wisconsin. Where was he taking them? What did he intend to do?

She'd gone along with him to protect Kaitlin, not to mention to get away from the rolling tear gas and flying bullets. But now, she was second-guessing her decision.

She and Kaitlin would likely be safer on their own. She trusted the police would protect them. Why wouldn't they?

Somehow, she needed to find a way to escape.

Caleb dragged a hand over his face as the SUV ate up the miles, and tried to think rationally. He didn't know who'd fired those shots at him, but if he hadn't picked up Kaitlin's stuffed giraffe, he'd be dead.

Leaving Kaitlin an orphan.

Somehow, he felt stupid for not realizing that whoever had killed his wife would still be out there somewhere, waiting for him. But the attempt on his life didn't make much sense. Why not try to plant more evidence to get him back behind bars? What would they gain from killing him?

"Where's Giffy?" he heard Kaitlin ask. The little girl had napped for a while but was obviously awake now.

"Right here, sweetheart." In the rearview mirror, he saw Kaitlin hug the stuffed giraffe close.

"Ah, Mr. O'Malley?" Noelle's voice was soft, almost hesitant. He hated seeing the shadow of fear in her eyes, but he didn't know how to reassure her he was innocent of the crime he'd been accused of. He could talk all he wanted, but without proof that he was being framed, there wasn't much he could do.

"Caleb," he corrected curtly. "Call me Caleb."

"Uh, sure. Caleb. It's past five-thirty and Kaitlin usually eats dinner about this time," she said with a hint of nervousness.

He flushed, squelching a flash of guilt. He should have realized that his daughter would need to eat soon. After fourteen long months in jail he'd forgotten how to be a father. "Sounds like a plan. What would you like?"

"Kaitlin, what do you want for dinner?" Noelle asked.

The little girl pulled her thumb out of her mouth. "Chicken bites."

In the rearview mirror he caught the fleeting grimace that passed over Noelle's face, but she readily agreed with Kaitlin's decision. "That would be great."

"Looks like there's a fast-food restaurant five miles ahead," he said, gesturing to a road sign. "We'll get something there."

"Thank you."

He swallowed a frustrated sigh. Noelle acted as if he was some sort of ogre keeping her and Kaitlin prisoner. Yet what could he have done differently? If he had left Kaitlin behind and something had happened to his daughter, he'd never have forgiven himself. No question he'd give up his life for Kaitlin.

And he couldn't bring himself to trust the police, either. Not when he fully believed that someone from his SWAT team had set him up for his wife's murder.

Feeling grim, he imagined that the cops were right now swarming Noelle's house, gathering evidence. What would they think when they found the slugs from a high-powered rifle and a canister of tear gas in her house? Would that prove his innocence? Or would they turn the whole thing around to somehow make him the bad guy?

He couldn't help believing the latter. It wouldn't be long before the killer was hot on their tail. He needed to figure out a good place to hide until he could find someone to trust.

Not that he could think of too many people he trusted at the moment. He'd put his faith in his lawyer, Jack Owens, but Jack had been the only person who'd known Caleb's plan of going to Noelle's house. Not that he could understand why Jack would try to kill him after working more than a year to set him free.

His wife's killer had clearly set him up to rot in prison for the rest of his life. And now that Caleb had been given a get-out-of-jail-free card, it was possible that the same person had tried to kill him. Unless his wife had other lovers who he didn't know about, someone who'd taken shots at him in an effort to seek revenge?

He sighed and turned off the highway, heading onto a side road leading to the popular fast-food restaurant. He pulled in and headed down the drive-through lane.

"I hav'ta go potty," Kaitlin announced.

He inwardly winced, feeling guilty for not anticipating his daughter's needs. He made a quick U-turn in the parking lot so he could pull into a spot located near the front of the building.

He slid out from behind the wheel but before he could

try to help Kaitlin out of her booster seat, Noelle took control, undoing the buckles to free his daughter. She carried Kaitlin out and set her down on the ground.

"I hav'ta go now!" Kaitlin said, rushing toward the door. Noelle sprinted to catch up, quickly capturing Kaitlin's hand.

"I'll take you to the bathroom, okay, sweetie?"

Caleb followed them inside, feeling like an outsider. He'd lost so much time with his daughter. The fact that she didn't want to be near him was like a knife to his heart.

Standing at the back of the lobby area, he stared blindly at the menu selections. Food wasn't nearly as important as keeping his daughter safe from harm. He felt exposed standing here in the middle of a fast-food joint, considering how just three hours ago, someone tried to kill him. Yet he'd kept a careful eye out to make sure they hadn't been followed.

But they weren't safe yet, not by a long shot.

Noelle and Kaitlin returned from the bathroom and he couldn't help smiling at the way his daughter was giggling.

"I had no idea public restrooms could be fun," he said with a smile.

Noelle shrugged. "She found the air hand-drying machine entertaining."

"So, Katydid, what would you like for dinner?" he asked, capturing his daughter's gaze. He hoped she remembered his pet name for her.

She tilted her head to the side and gave him an exasperated look. "I already tole you, chicken bites."

She hadn't reacted to the nickname, but at least she wasn't crying, either. He tried to take heart at the minor step forward. "Okay, one order of chicken bites. Noelle, what would you like?"

"I'll have a grilled chicken sandwich."

"What about to drink? I'll get Kaitlin some milk, but what would you like?"

"Water is fine."

He nodded and decided to order a thick cheeseburger for himself. Soon they had their food piled on a plastic tray. Noelle and Kaitlin picked out a small rectangle table and he made sure to sit where he could keep an eye on the door.

He found himself distracted by Kaitlin, who'd grown so much in the time he'd been stuck behind bars. Before he could dig into his food, Noelle surprised him by taking Kaitlin's hand in hers and bowing her head.

"Dear Lord, we thank You for providing this food for us to eat and we ask for Your protection and Your guidance in showing us the right path. Amen."

"Amen," his daughter echoed.

He paused, unsure of how he felt about the fact that Noelle was teaching his daughter to pray. He and Heather hadn't been particularly religious and he instinctively knew Heather would have been upset at Noelle's teaching Kaitlin about God. But he decided there were worst things than being a Christian so he didn't say anything. Although he couldn't help wondering what else Noelle had taught Kaitlin while he'd been gone.

He bit into his cheeseburger, enjoying the juicy taste he'd long been denied. He divided his attention between Kaitlin and the door. His daughter ate sparingly, spending more time playing with her chicken bites, pretending they were animals talking to each other. Regret burned in the back of his throat for the time he'd lost. He wanted nothing more than to gather his daughter into his arms and hold her close, but he'd rather cut off his arm than scare her again.

"Eat your dinner, Kaitlin," Noelle said in a soft but stern tone.

"Are we goin' home soon?" Kaitlin asked.

Noelle lifted her eyebrow and glanced at him. He cleared his throat and smiled. "We're going to spend the night in a motel. Won't that be fun?"

His daughter's big blue eyes, mirror images of her mother's, widened with excitement. "Wif a swimming pool?"

"I don't know, maybe." There were plenty of hotels with pools, but he'd wanted to find something small and off the main thoroughfares. Maybe he'd get lucky and find a small motel with an outdoor pool. After all, it was mid-June, warm enough for outdoor swimming. He was eager to gain whatever ground he could with his daughter. "But first you have to finish your dinner."

"Okay." She grinned saucily and popped another chicken bite into her mouth, smearing ketchup across her cheek. He was glad to see she was growing more at ease with him.

He reached for his napkin but Noelle was quicker, already wiping the red stain away. He curled his fingers into a helpless fist.

And couldn't help wondering if Noelle was really trying to help. Or if this was a subtle way of sabotaging his relationship with his daughter.

Noelle finished her sandwich about the same time as Caleb. She gathered all the trash into a neat pile on the tray while they waited for Kaitlin. When they'd first entered the restaurant, she'd considered asking one of the patrons for help, but there weren't many people inside.

And what if they simply looked at her as if she were crazy? Technically, Caleb had legal custody of his daughter, while she didn't have any right to the child. For now, she'd decided to go along with pretending to be a family.

The stark longing in Caleb's eyes as he gazed at his daughter made her wonder if she'd misjudged him. Clearly he loved Kaitlin and during the course of the meal she found herself torn between wanting to get as far away from him as she could and wanting to help him repair his relationship with the daughter who barely remembered him.

She couldn't imagine who'd tried to shoot him, but at least now the black truck that had trailed her for days made sense. Whoever was driving it must have been waiting for Caleb to arrive. If Caleb was truly innocent of the crime he'd been accused of, why would someone still want him dead? Was it possible he had really been framed? Or was that wishful thinking on her part?

"We need to go," Caleb said.

"All right," she agreed. Kaitlin was obviously finished with her food, so she quickly wiped off the little girl's sticky fingers and then stood up. Caleb took the tray of garbage and headed over to the trash can. Then he waited for her by the door, holding it open for the two of them.

They walked toward her car and as Caleb opened the back passenger door, she caught a glimpse of a police car pulling into the parking lot of the restaurant. She froze, wondering if she could manage to capture the cop's attention. Would the cop believe her story? Or would he run a check on Caleb only to find that he did have legal custody of his daughter?

"You're welcome to leave, but you won't take my daughter," Caleb warned, clamping his hand on her elbow to prevent her from leaving. "So make up your mind, and quick."

She hesitated, full of uncertainty.

"Just get Kaitlin into the car, all right?" he pressed.

"Uh, sure." She lifted Kaitlin into the booster seat. Her fingers were shaking so badly that she had trouble buckling the girl in.

When Kaitlin was safely secured in the seat she shut the door and made her way around to the other side, trying to see where the cop car was located. The officer had pulled into the drive-through lane and had his window rolled down as he perused the menu.

If she started screaming like a lunatic, would he help her?

"Sit up front next to me," Caleb said when she reached for the back door handle.

She felt trapped but since there was no way she was going anywhere without Kaitlin, she climbed into the front passenger seat.

When she glanced over to the police car, it was farther away, having moved forward to the next window.

Within moments Caleb drove back out onto the road, leaving the police car and any hope of getting help behind.

TWO

Noelle was grateful that after another two hours of driving, Caleb pulled off onto an exit that advertised a motel with a swimming pool.

The motel was small, but not so small that there weren't other guests, at least based on the cars in the parking lot. She was berating herself for not taking a chance by going to the police.

Too late now. She'd agreed to stay with him for Kaitlin's sake. Her own deep-seeded fears meant nothing compared to keeping the little girl safe from harm.

Caleb kept her close by his side, as if worried she might try something rash. She found his presence overwhelming. She wasn't used to being so close to a man, hadn't dated anyone in years. The three of them walked into the lobby together, and she knew he wanted to give the clerk the impression that they were a family, especially when he'd requested one room with two beds.

"How's the water in the pool?" Caleb asked the older man behind the desk as he paid in cash for the room. The guy barely glanced at his driver's license.

The guy shrugged. "Probably a bit on the cold side by now," he said in a disinterested tone. There was a small television behind the desk and his gaze kept straying back toward the baseball game he had on.

"Thanks," Caleb said cheerfully.

"Can we go swimming? Please?" Kaitlin asked.

"Soon," he promised, taking the room key and then holding the door open for Noelle and Kaitlin as they made their way back outside. There were two levels of the motel but Noelle noted their room was on the first floor, closest to the outdoor pool.

The room was nothing special, but it appeared clean enough. Kaitlin disappeared into the bathroom. When the child was out of earshot Noelle turned to Caleb. "Now what?" she asked in a low tone.

His enigmatic gaze didn't reveal much. "There must be spare clothes in that backpack that Kaitlin can use to swim in."

"There's one change of clothes, the rest is in her suitcase we left behind. And I don't have any other clothes and neither do you. She's too young to swim by herself."

"There's a strip mall a few miles down the street. We'll stop by tomorrow to pick up a few things," he said. "And the pool isn't that deep. At the very least she can dangle her feet in the water."

As annoyed as she was with him, she couldn't help appreciating the way he was trying so hard to make his daughter happy. But at the same time, she also wished he'd simply let them go.

Was he right in thinking that the person who'd shot at him would use Kaitlin to get to Caleb? Or was that just a handy excuse? She wished she knew.

Kaitlin came out of the bathroom and jumped up beside her on the bed. "Can we swim now, Noa? Puleeze?"

Looking down into Kaitlin's big blue eyes, she couldn't bear to disappoint the little girl. "Sure, sweetie."

"Why does she call you Noa?" Caleb asked, a small frown puckering his brow.

Did he resent their closeness? It certainly wasn't her fault he'd been arrested.

She dug in the backpack for a pair of shorts and a top that Kaitlin could use in lieu of a swimsuit. "Because she couldn't pronounce my name. Noa was as close as she could get to Noelle."

"How is it that you became her foster mother?"

She had no intention of giving him her life story. Especially since that would include confessing her horrible past along with her more recent failures. Trusting him as much as she had so far had been difficult enough. Under normal circumstances she avoided men, especially macho, dangerous types like Caleb. She forced a casual tone. "I'm your daughter's preschool teacher and happen to be licensed as a foster parent. I asked for custody and the state agreed."

If he was embarrassed that he didn't recognize her from the preschool, he didn't show it. She wasn't necessarily surprised that he hadn't remembered her, because his wife had been the one who'd come in to drop off and pick up Kaitlin, at least 80 percent of the time. The few times Caleb had come, he hadn't seemed to notice her.

She still remembered the last time she'd seen Heather, the day before she'd died. Caleb's wife had come in late on that Friday, almost twenty minutes past closing. Heather had looked nervous and hadn't been alone. There had been another man with her, who'd waited impatiently near the doorway.

It wasn't until after Heather's affair had hit the news that she'd understood what she'd seen that evening.

Tearing her thoughts away from the past, she turned

her attention to helping Kaitlin change her clothes into a shorts-and-top set.

"But this isn't my swimming suit," Kaitlin protested with a frown. "My swimming suit has sparkles."

"We left your swimming suit at home, remember?" she said patiently. "Do you want to check out the water or not?"

"I do! I do!" The little girl jumped up and down for emphasis.

"All right, let's go." She ducked into the bathroom, grabbed a towel off the rack and then came back out to take Kaitlin's hand in hers.

Caleb silently held the door open once again. *A criminal with manners,* she thought, fighting a sense of hysteria as they walked over to the pool area. He unlatched the fence, and she was surprised and a bit disappointed to find there weren't any other guests there.

Kaitlin ran over to the edge of the pool.

"Wait for me," Noelle called out, quickly taking off her sandals. "We have to check the water first."

She glanced over at Caleb, surprised to see he was taking off his running shoes, too. He then proceeded to roll his jeans halfway up his calves, which would have looked geeky on anyone else.

But there was nothing geeky about Caleb. He must have worked out while he was in jail because he was lean and muscular, without an ounce of fat to be seen. His dark hair was short and she wondered if that was by choice. Or if he'd been forced to get it cut.

Did they have barbers in jail?

He plopped down on the edge of the pool and put his feet in the water. "Come over and test the water, Katy-did."

Kaitlin hung back, staying next to Noelle. She urged

the little girl over, taking a seat on the edge of the pool next to Caleb, leaving enough room between them for Kaitlin. The little girl sat down and then shrieked when she put her feet in the water. "It's cold!"

"Probably because the sun is going down," Caleb said. "I bet it will be warmer tomorrow. See that plastic cover rolled up over there? They put that on at night, and in the morning the sun shines through the bubbles to warm up the water."

Kaitlin kicked her feet, giggling as she splashed the adults. Noelle tensed, but Caleb didn't yell or tell Kaitlin to stop. In fact, he playfully kicked his feet, too, mimicking his daughter.

"Can I go in farther, Noa? Can I?" Kaitlin pleaded.

"You can if you hold on to me," Caleb answered, holding out his hands in a nonthreatening gesture.

Noelle held her breath as Kaitlin silently stared up at her father. The lure of the water must have been more than she could resist, though, because she nodded.

Caleb gently lifted her up, as if she weighed nothing more than Kaitlin's stuffed giraffe, and propped his elbows on his knees for stability. Slowly he lowered Kaitlin into the water, her tiny hands clutching his forearms.

"It's c-c-cold," she said, her teeth chattering.

"Do you want to get out?" Caleb asked.

"N-no, not yet." Kaitlin wiggled around in the water, as if she could swim with her father holding her, and then scrunched up her nose when a bit of water splashed in her face. He grinned and lifted her up and down, like a bobber on the end of a fishing pole.

She watched Caleb play with his daughter, her reserve melting away. His smile softened his harsh features to the point it was difficult to imagine him doing anything as terrible as killing his wife.

"Okay, I think that's enough, Katydid," Caleb said, lifting her out of the water and setting her back on the edge of the pool. "Your lips are turning blue."

"I'll get the towel," Noelle murmured, glad to have an excuse to put some distance between them. Why did she suddenly doubt the image the media had portrayed? An eyewitness had watched Caleb kill his wife and then flee the scene.

An eyewitness who'd disappeared. Why? What did that mean?

She hid her confusion by wrapping Kaitlin up in the towel. The little girl snuggled against her and yawned.

"I think it's bedtime, young lady," she said, glancing up at Caleb. He nodded, rose to his feet and padded across the concrete to where he'd left his shoes and socks.

As they made their way back to the room, she reminded herself that it was easy to believe Caleb's father-of-the-year act because she hadn't seen him angry. She'd suffered at the hands of an angry man in the past and the last thing she wanted to do was to find herself in a similar situation with Caleb. So far, she had not seen any evidence of his so-called hair-trigger temper.

And silently prayed that she never would.

Caleb stretched out on the bed fully dressed, and stared up at the ceiling of the small motel room. Noelle and Kaitlin were snuggled together in the other bed, the one closest to the bathroom.

There were a few things he wanted to do, but he didn't dare leave until he knew they were both sound asleep. He was fairly certain Kaitlin was down for the count, but he sensed Noelle was fighting to stay awake. Finally her breathing deepened and he waited another hour just to be sure she was asleep before he quietly stood and made his way to the door.

He held his breath as he opened the door as silently as possible and slipped outside. Had the noise caused Noelle to wake up? He sincerely hoped not.

First, he needed to swap the license plates on Noelle's SUV. He drove down the road, looking for a car that he could use for the swap. He was afraid that anyone within the motel parking lot might notice, so he was determined to find a vehicle somewhere else.

About three miles down the road he spotted a tavern that suited his needs perfectly. He pulled up to a SUV similar to Noelle's and smiled grimly when he discovered the Illinois license plates. Even better. He made sure the tag was paid up, and then used his Swiss Army knife to swap the plates.

At least this way, he could buy some time if whoever shot at him had an APB out on Noelle's car. It wouldn't work forever, but he'd take what he could get.

He returned to the motel, relieved to have that task finished. He parked and shut off the car, but stayed in his seat as he turned on his cell phone to place a call to his lawyer, Jack Owens. It was well past midnight, but he didn't care. He wanted answers.

The phone rang several times before Jack answered. "O'Malley, where are you?" he asked in a sleep-laden voice.

"Somewhere safe. I'm sure you know by now that someone tried to kill me," he said. "What's going on?"

"I don't know, but the police want to talk to you, Caleb. They've been hounding me all evening."

"Too bad." The last thing he intended to do was to trust the police. Not after the way his SWAT teammates had been so eager to believe the worst about him. And there was a tiny voice in the back of his mind reminding him that Jack was the only person who'd known he was heading over to pick up his daughter. Granted anyone could have made a reasonable assumption, but still. "Did they find the slugs embedded in the house? And the canister of tear gas?"

"They haven't told me much," Jack confessed. "Other than they want to talk to you."

"Kind of hard to shoot at myself, don't you think?" he asked, trying not to sound as sarcastic as he felt. "I'd estimate the shooter was standing about a hundred and fifty yards away."

"I believe you. You're the sharpshooter. But you really do need to come back, at least long enough to give your statement," Jack pleaded. "After all, you have nothing to hide. You're the victim this time, remember?"

He wished it were that easy, but knew full well it wasn't. "What are they saying about Noelle Whitman and Kaitlin?" he asked, changing the subject.

"Not much, at least as far as I know. Although the police want to interview Ms. Whitman, too."

Of course they did. And despite the way he'd watched her pray over their meal, he wasn't ready to trust her completely, either. He sighed, feeling as if the weight of the world were on his shoulders. "I have to go. Let me know if you find out anything about the crime scene," he said. "I'll be in touch in a few days."

"Caleb—" Jack started, but Caleb pushed the button to end the call, and then turned off his phone not just to avoid further conversation with Jack but to preserve the battery life and to prevent anyone tracing him through the GPS.

For several long moments he stared sightlessly through the windshield of Noelle's SUV. He wanted to trust his lawyer—after all, Jack had been the only one to stick by him throughout the entire nightmare of being charged for murder. Of course, Caleb had paid the man a tidy sum of money to represent him, so that might not mean much. But he couldn't come up with any reason his own lawyer would want him dead.

No, somehow the attempt on his life outside Noelle's house had to be connected with Heather's murder. It was the only thing that made sense. Someone who was afraid he'd discover the truth? Someone who was feeling desperate, now that the so-called eyewitness had disappeared? And why had the guy disappeared? A sudden attack of cold feet about committing perjury? Or something more sinister?

He took a deep breath and slid out of the car, closing the door behind him as silently as possible. Using the magnetic key, he quietly opened the door and slipped inside. He stood for several long seconds, allowing his eyesight to adjust to the darkness and listening to make sure Noelle and Kaitlin were still asleep.

Reassured by the steady breathing, he ventured farther into the room, estimating the location of the bed.

And then nearly fell flat on his face when Kaitlin screamed.

Noelle bolted upright in bed and gathered the little girl close. "Shh, it's okay, sweetie. I'm here, it's okay," she crooned.

"What's wrong?" Caleb asked hoarsely.

"Nightmare. Shh, Kaitlin, please don't cry. It's okay, sweetie, you're fine. Everything's fine."

She felt the mattress dip as Caleb came over to sit beside them. "Is there anything I can do?" he asked softly.

"For night terrors? I'm afraid not," she responded,

still smoothing her hand down Kaitlin's back. After what seemed like ages, the little girl's screams subsided into hiccuping sobs, her tiny face still pressed tightly against her neck. "I'm sure she'll calm down soon."

There was a long pause as she rocked Kaitlin back and forth, still murmuring words of reassurance.

"She's done this before, hasn't she?" he asked.

"Yes, but not lately." *Not for over six months,* but she didn't tell him that. She'd suspected the gunfire, tear gas and subsequent wild ride out the back of her garage would bring them back. "Unfortunately, with everything that happened today, I'm not surprised they returned."

Please, Lord, bring peace to this sweet little girl. She's an innocent victim in all of this.

Noelle lost track of time as she held Kaitlin, waiting for her to fall asleep once again. When Kaitlin's breathing slowed and her tiny body went slack, she stopped rocking and gently lowered the child to the bed. Caleb moved away, and now that her eyes had adjusted to the darkness, she watched him scrub his hands over his face.

She knew just how helpless he felt; she'd experienced the same thing during those first few months that Kaitlin had come to live with her.

"Excuse me," she whispered, making her way into the bathroom. She used the facilities and splashed cold water on her face to brace herself before heading back out to face him.

Caleb had opened the curtains a half inch, allowing the light from the outside parking lot to shine into the room. He was seated on a chair near the window, holding his head in his hands.

He lifted his head when she approached. "This is my fault, isn't it?" he asked.

Why she wanted to make him feel better, she had no idea. "It's not your fault someone shot at you."

"I can't stand the thought of Kaitlin being afraid of me," he whispered.

"She's not," she whispered back. "After all, she let you hold her in the pool, remember?"

He shook his head. "She wanted to swim so badly I think she would have let anyone hold her."

Noelle sank down onto the chair next to him, unable to refute his logic. "She needs a little time, that's all."

He lifted his gaze to hers. "Maybe I can find a safe place for the two of you to stay for a while. Then I'll head off on my own to try and figure out who's trying to kill me."

As much as she wanted him to let them go, she couldn't seem to stop herself from arguing. "Don't you think that's a job for the police? They have more resources than you do."

"Not if they're in on it," he muttered. "Don't you understand? I can't trust the police, not after the way everything went down. The entire community thinks I'm guilty. And I can't take the chance the shooter will use my daughter to get to me."

"Who is the shooter? And why would anyone do something so terrible? I don't understand what's going on, Caleb."

He stared at her in the darkness, and she wished she could see his eyes more clearly. Strange that her earlier distrust of Caleb seemed to have faded in the wake of Kaitlin's nightmare.

"I don't understand what's going on, either," he said. "Other than someone wants to kill me. Likely the same person who killed my wife. And why wouldn't that person try to use Kaitlin? She's my one and only weakness.

Anyone who knows me, which includes all the guys on my former SWAT team, would know that I'd do anything to keep my daughter safe."

She wasn't sure what to say to that. "You really think someone on your team killed your wife?"

"Yes, I do. I've thought of nothing but Heather's murder for the fourteen months and it's the only theory that makes sense. I know you don't believe me, but I promise you I didn't kill her. I'd considered filing for divorce, when I discovered she was cheating on me, but I didn't kill her. And I especially wouldn't do that while Kaitlin was sleeping in her bedroom. I wasn't there that night because I'd moved into a motel room. And no matter what that neighbor claimed he saw, I did not go back to the house to kill Heather."

She'd known that Kaitlin being there the night of her mother's murder had been the source of the child's night terrors. The poor child had likely woken to the gunshots and had been found covered with blood in her mother's room.

After seeing Caleb interact with his daughter, she found it hard to believe everything had happened the way the eyewitness had claimed. That Caleb had killed his wife and then had run away from the house, carrying a gun and leaving his daughter behind.

A gun that still hadn't been found.

Not to mention an eyewitness who'd disappeared.

Had Caleb really been sleeping in a motel room while someone else killed his wife?

"You'd better try to get some sleep," he finally said.

"All right." She rose to her feet and crossed over to the bed she shared with Kaitlin.

But sleep was a long time coming, because for some

odd reason, she found she was beginning to believe Caleb was in fact innocent of the crime he'd been accused of.

But knowing that didn't reassure her the way she thought it would.

Because whoever had tried to kill Caleb outside her house was very likely still looking for him. And she was deeply afraid that the killer wouldn't hesitate to take the life of a woman and child, too, if necessary.

THREE

Caleb woke up after five hours of sleep, feeling surprisingly refreshed. Maybe because it was his first night of sleep as a free man. He'd never slept well in jail, too much noise from the other inmates and guards constantly making rounds. Even a low-budget motel room was better than what he'd left behind.

The sun was up, but it was still early, barely seven-thirty in the morning. Noelle and Kaitlin were sleeping in, so he quietly made his way to the bathroom, gently closing the door behind him. He felt better after a hot shower, but wished he had a razor and toothpaste.

He planned to make good on his promise to do some shopping right after breakfast. Then maybe they could take Kaitlin swimming again, before they had to hit the road. As much as he wanted to stay here another day, he didn't dare stick around in one spot for too long. He'd just have to find another motel with a pool for Kaitlin.

Remembering his daughter's nightmare made him frown. It had been the first hint of what his daughter had gone through emotionally and psychologically after his arrest. He was sincerely glad to know that Noelle had been there for Kaitlin the past fourteen months. The way she'd soothed his daughter last night during her nightmare had touched his heart.

Noelle was a much better mother than Heather had been.

The instant the thought sank in, he thrust it away. He closed his eyes and dragged his hands over his rough cheeks. The demise of his marriage hadn't been all Heather's fault and he needed to stop thinking negative thoughts about his former wife. No matter how she'd betrayed him, and violated their marriage vows, she hadn't deserved to be murdered.

He shoved the past away and finished cleaning up. When he emerged from the bathroom, Noelle was sitting at the side of the bed, finger-combing her hair. "Good morning," she whispered.

"Morning." The hint of fear that had shadowed her eyes since he arrived on her doorstep seemed to have vanished. He was afraid to hope that maybe, just maybe, she was starting to believe him. "I thought we'd get something to eat and then find a store. I'm sure you'd like some toothpaste as much as I would."

A shy smile bloomed on her face. "Yes, that would be wonderful."

Kaitlin opened her eyes and rolled onto her back, a tiny frown furrowing her brow as she looked around in confusion. "Noa?"

"I'm here, sweetheart," Noelle said as she pulled the little girl close and gave her a hug.

He wanted to give his daughter a hug, too, but stayed where he was, hoping she'd remember the way he'd held her in the pool rather than the way they'd escaped the gunman at Noelle's house. "Hey, Katydid, are you hungry?"

Kaitlin gazed at him solemnly before nodding her head. "Yes."

"Me, too," Noelle said. "Let's wash up in the bathroom first, okay, Kaitlin? Then we'll get some breakfast."

Kaitlin let go of Noelle and scrambled off the bed. She went into the bathroom and Noelle grabbed the pink backpack before following his daughter.

While he waited, he took out his wallet to double-check the amount of cash he had left. Thankfully Jack had stopped at the bank on the way home so that Caleb could draw out a chunk of his savings, partially to pay his legal fees along with having some cash to live on. Good thing, since staying alive was obviously a priority at the moment.

Heather had made a good living as a model before they'd gotten married, and after Kaitlin's birth she'd worked out like a maniac to get back in shape to resume her career. He'd tried to tell her she didn't need to keep modeling, but she'd insisted. The amount of money she made was more than what he made as a member of the SWAT team, but he'd rather Heather would have been content to do something else. It wasn't as if she was going to be able to model for the rest of her life. But she'd refused to consider a second career. He hadn't wanted to leave Kaitlin in the preschool center full-time, but Heather had insisted.

As a result of their combined incomes, they'd had a substantial amount of money saved up. Enough that he'd been able to continue paying the mortgage while he was behind bars. With Jack's help he'd listed the house on the market, but apparently no one was anxious to buy a home where a murder had taken place.

Not that he could blame them.

The amount of cash he had would probably only last

them a week, maybe more if he was frugal. He considered calling Jack for assistance in getting more money, but decided he'd wait until the following Monday. Considering it was a Saturday, there wasn't enough time to get back into Milwaukee before the banks closed. Besides, he didn't really want to head back into town so soon after leaving. Not when he suspected the cops would be looking for him and for Noelle's SUV.

He was sure to be a *person of interest* despite Jack's assurances that he was a victim. When he'd been arrested after Heather's death, he'd assumed that he'd be found innocent because he was. But then the eyewitness had stepped forward and he had no choice but to grapple with the possibility of spending the rest of his life behind bars.

No way was he making the same mistake twice.

The bathroom door opened, letting a cloud of steam into the room. Noelle's hair was damp from her shower, and Kaitlin was wearing her previous clothes. He quickly stuffed the money back into his wallet and turned toward them. "Ready for breakfast?"

"Absolutely," Noelle said cheerfully. For a moment her gaze locked on his and he wished he knew what she was thinking. Had she changed her mind about him at all? Or was that wishful thinking? And why did he care?

"Let's go," he said, crossing over to open the motel room door. Kaitlin eagerly dashed outside, as if the nightmare from last night was already forgotten. Noelle seemed content to walk beside him.

After they reached the car, Noelle helped Kaitlin into her booster seat before taking her place beside him up front without his having to ask. He headed down the road to a well-known chain restaurant that served breakfast, trying not to read too much into Noelle's small gesture of trust.

No matter how much he wanted to.

* * *

Noelle finished her breakfast, a yummy veggie omelet, before she realized that she hadn't once looked for an opportunity to escape.

Was she crazy to put her trust in Caleb? She sipped her coffee, trying to sort out her feelings.

Caleb's despair last night hadn't been faked. He'd truly felt awful about Kaitlin's nightmare. But did the fact that he loved his daughter make him innocent of the crime he'd been arrested for? Of course not.

So why did she suddenly believe him?

She closed her eyes for a moment and prayed. *Dear Lord, I don't know what to believe. Please help guide me. Please show me the way.*

A sense of peace settled over her and she realized that if Caleb had intended to hurt them, he would have done that already. Instead he'd done nothing but provide food and shelter. Not to mention, finding a pool to make his daughter happy.

Even now, he was coloring the paper cartoon place mat with Kaitlin, as if he didn't have a care in the world.

"No, Daddy, purple," Kaitlin insisted, shoving the green crayon aside. "Not green, purple."

"You're right, Katydid, purple is way prettier than green," Caleb agreed.

Noelle hid a smile behind her coffee mug. If she wasn't seeing the way he tried so hard to bond with his daughter with her own eyes, she wasn't sure she would have believed it. Especially when she hadn't watched Caleb interact with his daughter very much before he'd been accused of murder.

"Kaitlin, why don't you finish your scrambled eggs and bacon before they get cold," she suggested.

"We're almost done," Kaitlin muttered, filling in the

last of the cartoon character's bright purple dress. "See?" She held the paper up high. "Isn't it pretty?"

"Very pretty," she agreed. Caleb set down his crayon and reached for his own cup of coffee.

"Here, this is for you, Daddy." In a surprise gesture, Kaitlin handed the picture to Caleb and then picked up a piece of bacon.

"Thanks, Katydid," Caleb murmured in a husky tone. For a moment she thought there was a glint of tears in his eyes, but then it was gone. He gave Kaitlin a broad smile and carefully set the place mat in the center of the table, where it wouldn't get stained with food or drink. "This is the best present, ever."

She simply couldn't believe a man who cared so much about his daughter that he nearly cried after getting a picture from her was cold and callous enough to kill his ex-wife. In the past twenty-four hours, there'd been no sign of his so-called hair-trigger temper, either.

At this point, she had no reason not to give him the benefit of the doubt.

"Do you want anything more?" Caleb asked.

"No way, I'm stuffed," Noelle murmured, sitting back in her chair and feeling a bit guilty at how much she'd eaten. "That was delicious. Thanks, Caleb."

"You're welcome." He quickly finished his own meal, and then gestured for the waitress to bring the bill. He glanced at the amount and pulled out his wallet, leafing through the bills.

For the first time since this mad escape had started she found herself wondering how long they could stay on the run like this. She didn't have her purse, so she couldn't help pay for anything. What would happen when they ran out of cash? What if they messed up and the shooter who'd tried to kill Caleb found them?

She shivered, suddenly cold. Should she tell Caleb about the black truck that had been following her in the days prior to his release? Should she tell him about the man who'd accompanied his wife to pick up Kaitlin the Friday evening before she'd died? She'd told the police, but since she didn't have a name, there wasn't much they could do. The officer she spoke with assumed the guy was the same man Heather was having an affair with.

Wasn't it possible that man had killed Heather, rather than Caleb?

"Are you all right?" Caleb asked with a slight frown.

"Sure," she said, forcing a smile. The way he seemed to be tuned in to her emotions shouldn't make her believe in him even more. But it did. She reminded herself that Caleb wasn't her type. She didn't date men, especially handsome men. There was no way she should even think about Caleb on a personal level. Trusting a man enough to have a relationship was far too difficult for her.

"All finished, Katydid?" Caleb asked his daughter.

The little girl nodded and pushed her plate away. She'd eaten most of her food this morning, which gave Noelle some encouragement. Maybe if they kept things calm today, the little girl wouldn't suffer another night terror at bedtime.

They left the restaurant and stopped at the strip mall that was only a couple of miles away. Despite her concerns about money, Caleb seemed determined to get them each a change of clothes, including sweatshirts for the cooler nights, swimsuits and toiletries. Kaitlin was thrilled to have another sparkly swimsuit, jumping up and down with excitement when Caleb agreed to buy it for her. Noelle winced at the total, but he readily paid in cash.

It wasn't until they were walking back out to the parking lot, with Kaitlin skipping between them, that she noticed the license plates on her car. She stopped abruptly and stared.

Caleb instantly noticed her reaction. "Noelle, I only swapped them to keep us safe."

Logically she knew that, but he'd broken the law just the same. Apprehension swelled in her chest. "What if we get caught?"

His gaze was full of empathy. "Please try to trust me in this. I won't do anything to hurt you or Kaitlin. We'll take Kaitlin swimming and then hit the road. We'll be far away from here soon enough."

She took a ragged breath and gave a jerky nod. When Caleb opened the back of her car she stored the bag inside, hoping he didn't notice the way her hands were shaking.

Never in her life had she committed a crime. She always followed the rules. As a preschool teacher she took her job as being a role model for her students seriously. Granted she wasn't perfect. After all, she'd failed her previous foster child. She'd thought for sure she was getting through to the youngster but Stephanie had run away and had been found dead of a drug overdose.

No matter how much she'd prayed for peace, Noelle still carried the guilt over Stephanie's death. She'd done her best to make amends by helping Kaitlin.

She lifted Kaitlin into her booster seat and wondered if she'd made a grave mistake by trusting her instincts as far as Caleb was concerned.

Caleb glanced over at Noelle for the third time in five minutes, wishing she would say something. Anything. But she didn't. She merely sat there, looking devastated.

The shadow of fear was back in her eyes and he knew that his actions had put it there.

He shouldn't care what she thought about him, but he did. For so long, no one had believed him. Not the D.A. Not his teammates. Certainly not the media. He wasn't sure that Jack had really believed him, despite what the lawyer had claimed.

Even his closest friend, Declan Shaw, hadn't believed him.

So why was he surprised that Noelle, a virtual stranger, was suddenly acting as if he deserved to go back to prison?

The silence between them stretched as they made their way back to the motel. Most of the cars that had been parked outside were gone, probably because it was near the designated checkout time.

But he wasn't leaving until Kaitlin had a chance to swim. He parked in front of their room and slid out from behind the wheel. "Why don't you change into your swimsuits and I'll meet you out at the pool?" he suggested.

"Yay! I getta swim in my sparkly suit!" Kaitlin shrieked. He smiled grimly. At least one of them was happy.

"Sure." Noelle's less than enthusiastic response made him feel bad, but there wasn't much he could do to change what he'd done. Especially since he wasn't about to apologize for swapping out the plates. As far as he was concerned it was a small price to pay for keeping his daughter safe.

He carried the bag inside and then left them to change. He walked down to the office, relieved to see a woman sitting behind the counter, rather than the crabby old guy. He waited for her to finish with another couple who were checking out before he stepped up to the counter.

"Hi, we're in room twelve and we're checking out today, but would you mind if we did a late checkout so my daughter can swim before we leave? It would really mean a lot to her."

The woman scowled and shook her head. "Rules are rules. I'm afraid I'll have to charge you an extra fee for a late checkout."

He narrowed his gaze, but didn't bother arguing with her. He wondered what she and the old man had to be so crabby about anyway? "Fine, I'll load up the car now, then. Here's the amount we owe." He handed over the cash, tapping his foot impatiently as she took her time counting out the bills.

"Leave your key in the room," she instructed.

"I will." He turned and left, trying not to be annoyed. The girls were finished changing by the time he arrived. Noelle had a towel draped over her shoulders. "We'll just head out to the pool, okay?"

"Sure. We have to pack our stuff and vacate the room, so I'll be down in a few minutes."

Noelle didn't meet his gaze, but took Kaitlin's hand and headed outside. He quickly changed into a pair of swim trunks and a T-shirt before putting everything they'd purchased back in the plastic bag. He moved the car so that it wasn't right in front of the room, and parked it off to the far side of the parking lot, but within view of the pool. Then he took the bag to the pool area with him, figuring they could change their clothes in the restrooms located in the small building adjacent to the swimming area.

When he arrived he found Noelle and Kaitlin in the shallow end of the pool. Noelle was holding Kaitlin as she moved around in the water, while his daughter giggled and splashed.

He wished he was the one holding his daughter. He'd been secretly thrilled when she'd given him the coloring picture at the restaurant, but that brief moment of closeness seemed to have vanished.

And he would have done anything to bring it back.

He set their bag off to the side and joined them in the water, swimming laps while Noelle and Kaitlin played. After about an hour, he noticed his daughter was shivering and decided it was time for them to leave.

"But I don't wanna leave," Kaitlin wailed.

Noelle wrapped a towel around his daughter. "Kaitlin, you're shivering and your lips are blue. Let's go and change our clothes, okay?"

"B-but I'm n-not c-cold," Kaitlin protested, despite the way her teeth were chattering.

He had to smile at his daughter's stubborn streak. He had no idea how much she enjoyed the water, and he knew that he needed to find another hotel with a pool. Maybe if he acted as if this was nothing more than a fun vacation, she wouldn't have any more nightmares.

He took his own clothes inside the men's room and quickly changed. When he returned he wrapped his wet things in one of the smaller plastic bags.

Noelle and Kaitlin emerged from the women's room a few minutes later. "Here, I'll take your wet things," he said.

"Thanks," Noelle murmured as she handed over their wet clothes. Some of the tension seemed to have eased between them as she lifted her face to the sun. "Feels good to be warm."

"I know." He felt bad about dragging them away from the cozy motel, but he couldn't help the nagging feeling that they needed to keep moving. Even though he'd changed the license plates, it wasn't as if they still couldn't be found. For all he knew, the guy whose plates he swapped with had already informed the authorities. The cops could already be, right now, looking for the stolen tags he'd put on Noelle's car.

"No, I don't wanna go for a ride!" Kaitlin ran in the opposite direction, toward the plastic deck chairs lining the far side of the pool. Today, Noelle had dressed her in purple, his daughter's favorite color, with matching purple barrettes in her hair. Her cleft chin was thrust forward in a stubborn way that made him smile. Maybe he was a tad biased but he thought Kaitlin was the cutest kid on the planet.

Noelle let out an exasperated sigh at his adorable daughter's antics.

"Do you want me to get her?" he offered.

"No, I'll do it." Noelle walked slowly over to where Kaitlin stood, halfway hidden behind a deck chair. He lifted the plastic bag over his shoulder and followed.

A loud explosion caused him to instinctively duck and rush over to where Noelle and Kaitlin were standing. "Are you okay?" he asked hoarsely.

Kaitlin was crying but Noelle nodded. "Look!" she said with a gasp, pointing over his shoulder.

He turned and stared in shock at the ball of fire that engulfed Noelle's SUV.

Horror seeped through his bones. If not for Kaitlin's refusal to go along with them, they all would have been killed!

FOUR

Noelle couldn't tear her gaze away from the terrible black smoke and orange flames obscuring her car. How could this happen? Who had blown up her car? How had they been found?

"Come on, we have to get out of here!" Caleb picked up Kaitlin. "Grab the bag," he said as he headed over toward the fence. She picked up their meager belongings and hurried after him, trying to think logically.

"We can't just leave!" she whispered.

"Yes, we can. Whoever lit up your car could still be around." Caleb's terse tone made it clear he wasn't about to be swayed by any argument. "You go over the fence first, and I'll hand Kaitlin over."

She hadn't crawled over a fence since she was a teenager on the run from her foster home, but fear was a strong incentive. Caleb gave her a boost and she scrambled up and over. When she was safe on the other side, he lifted Kaitlin up and held her over the other side until Noelle had her. When she set the child on her feet, he tossed her the bag. Within moments he'd vaulted the fence and was standing beside her.

"See that outcropping of trees over there?" he asked in a low tone.

The trees were about fifty yards away. "Yes."

"I'll take Kaitlin. You take the bag. Keep your head down and run as fast as you can."

Miraculously Kaitlin didn't put up a fuss when Caleb scooped her into his arms. Noelle grasped the bag, took a deep breath and ran.

She stayed hunched over as much as possible, bracing herself for the sound of gunfire. She could feel Caleb's warm breath on her back as he ran behind her. When they reached the relative safety of the trees, she stopped and bent over to catch her breath.

"We have to keep going," Caleb urged, lightly grasping her arm. "Follow me."

She swallowed hard and nodded. She followed in his wake, running as best she could, darting between the trees with the plastic bag bumping against her legs along the way. She toyed with the idea of dumping it but figured she'd hang on as long as she could.

The woods ended abruptly in front of a cornfield. The stalks of corn weren't very high, but Caleb went into the narrow path between the rows regardless. She followed, darting a glance over her shoulder.

She didn't see anyone following them, but then again, she hadn't seen anyone before her car blew up, either. What choice did they have but to put as much distance between themselves and the motel as possible?

Strangely enough, she trusted Caleb to lead them to safety.

The wailing sounds of police sirens split the air and she saw Caleb tense before he increased the pace. She was already running as fast as she could, but she struggled to keep up. She wasn't a runner by nature. She hated jogging.

"This way," Caleb said as he veered off to the right.

There was an old farmhouse up ahead. She instinctively slowed. Why on earth would he risk going to a farmhouse? There had to be people living there, otherwise who'd planted the corn?

"Wait," she said between gasping breaths. "What are you doing?"

"I've been watching the place for a few minutes now. It looks pretty dilapidated. So far, I haven't seen anything indicating someone is living there," Caleb explained. "Once we're at the farmhouse we can rest for a few minutes."

She was apprehensive about following him but as they approached, she relaxed as the state of disrepair became more obvious. The wood siding that had once been a light green or yellow, hard to tell as it hadn't been painted in at least a decade, and several windows were broken. The yard was seriously overgrown with tall grass and megaweeds. The front porch was sagging so badly she had to assume the boards were rotting away underneath. There was no indication anyone was living there, and Caleb led them around to the back of the house, where there was plenty of shade providing relief from the sun. He gently set Kaitlin on her feet and the little girl rushed over to Noelle.

Noelle hugged her close and sank down into the long grass. *Thank You, Lord, for saving us!*

Caleb knew Kaitlin and Noelle needed some time to rest and recover, but he couldn't help feeling nervous as he glanced around to make sure they weren't followed. He'd ditched his cell phone back in the cornfield, not a big loss as the thing was out of battery anyway, but still, he wouldn't be happy until they were far away from here. The sirens had gone silent and he assumed that meant the police and the fire trucks had reached the motel. How long before the cops fanned out to look for them? Surely the desk clerk would be able to give adequate descriptions. Of him, for sure, although now that he thought about it, only the old man had seen Noelle and Kaitlin.

Still, they needed to get to safety. But how? The odds of getting away on foot weren't good. Especially since he would have to carry Kaitlin.

Squinting at their surroundings, he searched for familiar landmarks. When he recognized the buildings way off in the distance, he realized he'd headed in the same direction as the strip mall where they'd gone shopping earlier that morning. The mall provided at least one opportunity. As a cop he didn't like breaking the law, but what else could he do? If he didn't steal a car they'd never survive.

Oddly enough, he didn't like the thought of disappointing Noelle, either, but their safety was more important than worrying about his ridiculous feelings. He'd do whatever it took to keep them safe.

"I'm thirsty," Kaitlin said.

Regret welled in his chest. "I'm sorry, Katydid, but I'll get you some water as soon as possible, okay?"

"What's the plan?" Noelle asked with a weary smile.

He had to admit she'd held up through their mad dash through the woods like a trouper. "The mall where we shopped earlier today is a couple of miles down the road to the north," he said, indicating the general direction with a wave of his hand. "I think that's our best option."

Her gaze was troubled as she looked up at him. "We're not going to get very far without a car, are we?" she asked, a note of defeat in her tone.

"We'll think of something," he assured her. No point

in worrying about the next step until they had to. "Are you ready to keep going?"

"Sure." She stood and picked up the plastic bag. "Let's go."

He buried a flash of admiration for her strength and determination as he looked at Kaitlin. "Do you want to ride on my shoulders, Katydid?"

His daughter regarded him steadily for a moment and he hoped she might remember when he'd carried her like that when they attended the state fair a few short weeks before his wife's murder and his nightmare had begun. How he longed for those days. After what seemed like forever, she nodded and held up her arms. "Up!" she commanded.

His heart swelled with love as he put his hands around her tiny frame, lifted her up and set her gently on his shoulders. She clutched at his head, her tiny fingers finding his ears as a way to hang on when he started walking.

He ignored the discomfort, too happy to know his daughter was finally getting over her fear of him.

"Look, Daddy, birdies!" Kaitlin exclaimed.

"I see them, Katydid."

"Caleb, the road is over there," Noelle said, waving to the right.

"I know, but we'll save time if we cut through the cornfields." Being careful not to dislodge his daughter, he swept his gaze around the area, making sure they weren't attracting attention. "I'm guessing this farmland is being leased out to someone. It would explain the abandoned farmhouse."

"I guess you could be right. But, Caleb, why didn't the license plate swap work?" Noelle asked in a low tone. "Is it possible we were being followed the whole time?"

He let his breath out in a sigh. "I guess anything's

possible, but I can't see how I would have missed a tail. And if someone had followed us, why wait so long to make a move? We'd been at the motel for over twenty-four hours. There was plenty of time to go after us then." The more he thought about it, the more he realized how unlikely that was. "No, I can't believe we were followed."

"Then how did they find us?" she persisted.

Admitting his lack of poor judgment wasn't easy. "I made a mistake," he admitted in a grim tone.

"What mistake?"

"Last night, I called my lawyer, Jack. I thought I kept the call short enough, but considering what happened, I have to assume that he managed to get a trace on me."

"But why? Why would your lawyer do something like this?" she asked.

"Giddyup, Daddy," Kaitlin said, kicking her heels. "You're my horsey!"

The interruption made him chuckle, despite the seriousness of their situation. "This horsey isn't going any faster, Katydid. You might fall off." He glanced over at Noelle. "I don't know why Jack would do something like this," he said in a low tone. "It doesn't make any sense, especially since he worked so hard to get me released from jail."

Noelle switched the bag over to her other hand and he knew the bag was getting heavy. "Could someone else have tapped into your lawyer's phone to trace you here?"

He turned the possibility over in his mind. "A cop would have the technology and the equipment to do that," he said slowly. "I'm already convinced the guy who took a shot at me outside your house is someone from the team. That was a long but unerringly accurate shot."

"Except he missed," she said.

"Only because of Giffy," he muttered wryly.

"Or maybe because God has other plans for you," she persisted. "I'm so thankful God has been watching over us."

He wasn't sure what to say to that, so he kept silent. Was God watching over them? Watching over Noelle and Kaitlin, maybe, but him? Doubtful.

His shoulders were feeling the strain of carrying Kaitlin over the uneven turf so he kept his sights focused on the shopping mall. He didn't want to point out that God wasn't going to be too happy with him after he hot-wired a car.

Because truthfully, Noelle's disappointment would hurt more than anything God could dish out.

Noelle's arm muscles were screaming in protest from lugging their bag of belongings, but since Caleb was carrying Kaitlin she refused to complain.

She tried to keep focused on getting to safety. The buildings making up the shopping mall were slowly but surely getting closer. Once again, Caleb had saved her life. She'd never depended on a man before, not even when she was a teenager on the run from a physically abusive foster home. To this day she thanked God for sending her to a women's shelter run by Abigail Carrington. Abby had helped her turn her life around. She never would have gotten her GED and gone on to college if not for Abby's support.

After getting her preschool job and buying her very first home, she decided to try and give back to the community, the way Abby had given so selflessly to her. So she'd gone through the red tape of becoming a foster parent and had opened her home to Stephanie, a troubled young girl who'd been in rehab for drug abuse at the tender age of thirteen.

She veered away from thoughts of Stephanie; the pain of losing the young girl was still too raw even after two years. She hated knowing how badly she'd failed the young girl.

"Are you okay up there, Katydid?" Caleb asked.

"I wanna get down," Kaitlin whined.

"All right." Caleb stopped and carefully lifted the little girl off his shoulders. He held Kaitlin in his arms but she squirmed.

"I wanna walk by myself," she said with a pout.

Caleb shot her a helpless look and Noelle smiled and nodded. "I'm sure she'll be okay for a while."

"Here, I'll carry our stuff, then," he said, reaching for the bag. Their fingers brushed and clung as she untangled her fingers from the plastic.

"Thanks," she said breathlessly, avoiding his gaze. What was wrong with her? She should be immune to men, especially a guy like Caleb. She'd only had one boyfriend during college and that relationship had ended after a few short months because she just couldn't bring herself to trust Daniel. He quickly moved on to someone else, which convinced her she'd made the right decision. What she didn't know about men would fill an entire library.

She reminded herself that Caleb had been married to Heather, a beautiful, striking model with a slender figure and long, silky blond hair. He'd never be interested in someone plain, like her. And she should be absolutely glad about that.

So why wasn't she?

Stress. It had to be stress making her think these crazy thoughts. Stress of being on the run from someone who'd tried to kill them. Twice. Any normal woman would be stressed under these circumstances, right? Right.

Yet she couldn't deny that being with Caleb like this was far better than those horrible weeks she'd been on the streets alone back when she was seventeen.

"Hey, don't worry, we're almost there," Caleb said in an encouraging tone.

She realized she must have been scowling, so she relaxed her features. "I know."

"So far there's no sign of the police searching for us," he added. "I have to admit I'm a little surprised."

"Me, too. I thought they'd bring out the bloodhounds," she joked.

"Be glad they didn't," he said soberly.

Kaitlin was skipping ahead but she tripped and fell, letting out a screech. "Owwwieee!"

Noelle rushed over and scooped the girl up. "Shh, it's okay, sweetheart. Let me see. There now, there's no blood. It's okay. You're okay."

Thankfully Kaitlin's cries diminished to mere sniffles when she saw that indeed there was no blood. Noelle picked Kaitlin up, intending to carry the child for a little while.

"I can take her," Caleb offered. "She's too heavy for you to carry for long."

She reluctantly handed Kaitlin over, knowing he was right. Their bag of clothing and toiletries wasn't very heavy, either, at first but after a mile it had felt like a ton of bricks.

They were only twenty feet away from the mall parking lot now, and as they approached she noticed there was a big chartered bus parked in the center of the lot. And then she saw the soft-drink vending machine. Just seeing the cold drinks inside made her keenly aware of how parched she was.

"First stop, water," she said to Caleb as their footsteps hit the pavement.

"I'm with you," he murmured. He set Kaitlin down again, but this time held on to his daughter's hand so she couldn't run off as they crossed the parking lot.

As Caleb fed dollar bills into the vending machine, Noelle couldn't help watching the bus. There appeared to be several elderly people nearby, making her wonder if they'd come here on some sort of senior shopping trip.

"Here," Caleb said, handing her an ice-cold water bottle.

"Thanks. Kaitlin, do you want a drink?" she asked as she unscrewed the cap.

"Yes." Kaitlin tried to grab the water, but she held firm, so it wouldn't spill as the child took several big gulps. When the little girl was finished, she took a long sip herself.

"Wow, that hit the spot," Caleb murmured as he re-capped his water. "Why don't you two rest in the shade for a while? I'll be back soon."

Back? Where was he going? And then she knew he intended to steal a car. "Caleb, wait." She reached out to grasp his arm to prevent him from leaving. His skin was so hot she was half-afraid she'd be seared by the touch. Yet she refused to let go. "Why don't you let me talk to the bus driver first?"

"The bus driver?" he repeated. He looked over and frowned. "Noelle, that's a private bus, chartered for a specific event. There's no way they're going to give us a ride," he protested.

She knew the odds weren't good, but she didn't care. "Have faith, Caleb. At the very least it can't hurt to ask. Wait here a moment, okay?"

She could tell he didn't want to let her go over there

alone, but really after everything they'd been through it wasn't as if a bus driver and an elderly woman presented any sort of danger. Wishing she wasn't quite so hot and sweaty, she walked over to where the bus driver, a bald man who looked to be in his mid-sixties, was talking to a woman who was probably a decade older. From the gist of the conversation it appeared they were intending to leave soon.

Please, Lord, guide me through this.

"Hi there," she greeted them warmly. "My name is Noelle and we had a little car trouble a few miles back. Is there any way you would consider giving us a ride to wherever you're headed? We'd be so grateful."

"That's against the rules," the bus driver said quickly. "Sorry."

"Oh my dear, that's terrible," the elderly woman said with clear sympathy. "Do you want to borrow my phone to call a tow truck?"

"No, thanks, we really can't afford a tow truck and the car wasn't really worth much anyway," Noelle said sadly. She forced a smile and glanced again at the bus driver. If she could convince him to take them along, she thought for sure the elderly woman wouldn't mind. "I understand it's against the rules, but Kaitlin is only five and she's exhausted and hungry. We aren't asking you to go out of your way. Please?"

"That's not an option," he said firmly.

She swallowed a frustrated sigh. She had no idea what she could say to make this stubborn old man change his mind.

"Look, Harry, give this poor girl a break, will you? She's a nice Christian woman," the elderly woman said.

Noelle's jaw dropped open. "How did you know?" she asked.

The elderly woman gave her arm a gentle pat. "You're wearing a cross around your neck, my dear," she said in a soothing tone. "Now, Harry, what can it hurt to give this nice family a ride back to Madison? Three additional people aren't going to make one bit of difference to you. We've already paid you for the trip, haven't we?"

The old man scowled and scratched his jaw. "Don't see what good a ride will do, they have to get a tow truck eventually," he groused.

"What do you care if they do or they don't?" the elderly woman asked with exasperation. "Now, listen here, Harry, giving these young folks a helping hand is the right thing to do. Now, are you going to give them a ride or not?"

The bus driver must have realized he'd soon be outnumbered because he let out a huff and threw up his hands. "Okay, okay. I'll give them a ride."

Relief threatened to buckle Noelle's knees. "Oh, thank you! Thank you so much!"

"My name is Lydia Rawlings," the elderly woman said. "But you can call me Lydia. Now bring that cute little girl and that handsome husband of yours over and introduce us properly."

Husband? Noelle blinked in surprise, but didn't correct Lydia's assumption as she gestured for Caleb and Kaitlin to come over. Caleb's gaze was questioning as he approached.

She wet her lips nervously. "Caleb, I'd like you to meet Lydia Rawlings, who has graciously agreed to give us a ride to Madison. Lydia, this is Caleb and Kaitlin."

"Pleased to meet you, ma'am," Caleb said, offering his hand. "We're very grateful for the lift."

"Well, the Lord always finds a way to provide, doesn't He?" Lydia said with a laugh. "It's a pleasure to meet you, too, such a beautiful family. Now go ahead and climb inside. I can see the rest of the group is already making their way over."

Caleb's gaze clashed with hers and she lifted her shoulder in a tiny shrug in response to his unspoken question. She hadn't told Lydia they were a family and certainly it wasn't her fault the woman had jumped to that conclusion.

But as she climbed inside the blessed coolness of the bus, she found herself wishing they were a real family, instead of a make-believe one.

FIVE

Caleb followed Noelle and Kaitlin to the back of the bus, taking the seat directly behind the one they slid into together. He had to admit being very surprised Noelle had managed to convince the bus driver to take them along. And he was glad he didn't have to steal a car.

At least not yet.

Many of the elderly patrons of the bus filed in behind them, greeting the newcomers as they took their seats. Noelle chatted cheerfully, giving a good impression that they had nothing to hide as she thanked them again for allowing them to ride along.

Now that they were relatively safe, he couldn't help trying to figure out how they'd been tracked to the motel. Jack Owens had to be the leak. There was no other explanation. Caleb had kept his phone off, turning it on to make the one call to Jack, before shutting the phone down again.

Grimly, he knew if they'd checked out of the motel on time, hitting the road as he'd initially intended, they would have been driving along the interstate when the vehicle exploded. He wished he could go back and review the wreckage to look for proof. The more he thought about it, he had to assume the explosive device had been on some sort of timer. Because if someone had been keeping them under surveillance, that person would have made sure the three of them were tucked inside the SUV before the blast.

He scrubbed his hands over his face. If he hadn't insisted on taking Kaitlin for a swim, they would all be dead. Mission accomplished for the bad guy.

But why? That was the part he couldn't quite figure out. Obviously this had to be linked to his wife's murder, but he was having trouble connecting the dots. Other than the fact that whoever had killed his wife must be worried that Caleb would figure it out. Avoiding life in prison was a strong motive for the bad guy to kill him.

Unfortunately he really didn't have a clue who that person was. Someone from the SWAT team, sure, but which one? They all had experience with explosives so it was not as if the bombing of the SUV was a good clue. Most of them were sharpshooters, too. Although he figured he could cross a couple of the guys off the sharpshooter list. Declan had been one of his best friends but the guy couldn't hit the center of a target at one hundred and fifty feet if his life depended on it. Declan had other skills for sure, including nerves of steel when it came to defusing bombs. But as a sharpshooter? No way.

The thought of Deck making a bomb and sticking it under their vehicle made him feel sick to his stomach. He and Deck had trained together. Deck had been the best man at his wedding.

Had his best friend betrayed him?

He stared out the tinted windows, watching the elderly shoppers making their way toward the bus. They would be on the road soon, which suited him just fine.

But his gut twisted when a squad car rolled into the parking lot of the shopping mall.

Slouching down in his seat, he silently willed the elderly shoppers to hurry. The bus was more than half full, but these people were moving slower than snails, stopping and chatting along the way.

He could tell Noelle had seen the squad car, too, when she shot him a panicked look over her shoulder. He silently shook his head, indicating there was nothing they could do but to wait and hope the bus driver would get on the road. Soon. Thankfully the tinted windows would help hide them.

But what if the cops came onto the bus to search for them? They were sitting ducks here in their seats. He couldn't bear to think about it.

Honestly he was surprised it took the cops this long to fan out and search for them. He'd kept a keen eye out the entire trip here from the farmhouse to make sure the cops weren't following their tail. The only rational explanation was that they'd needed to get the fire under control first, to verify they weren't actually inside the car.

Unfortunately, the cops were here now.

He couldn't tear his gaze from the squad car, tracking its progress as it headed toward the storefront.

Hurry, hurry! he silently urged the shoppers. The squad car slowed to a stop and two deputies stepped out, both holding photos in their hands.

Pictures of him, and possibly Noelle and Kaitlin, too. A wave of helpless anger washed over him. He should have realized there were cameras in the lobby of the motel. These days there were cameras everywhere. He was trained as a cop, an elite member of the SWAT team. Being in jail for the past year was no excuse. If he didn't get his head in the game, he'd get them all killed.

One of the deputies turned and glanced over at the bus. He was saying something, but Caleb couldn't figure out what. He clenched his jaw so tight he was surprised he didn't crack a molar. There were only a couple of elderly shoppers left, but the very last woman was walking with excruciating slowness, leaning heavily on her cane for support.

Come on! Hurry!

He wondered if the bus driver hadn't somehow felt his intense vibe to leave as the older guy stepped off the bus to give the woman with her cane a helping hand. The second deputy gestured toward the drugstore where they'd stopped yesterday to pick up their toiletries. After a long heartbeat, the two men went inside the store.

Grimly, he realized the female clerk would likely identify them to the cops, as she'd made a big fuss over Kaitlin at the time. And they'd only been there a few hours ago.

The cane woman finally dropped into a seat toward the front of the bus. The driver stood in the aisle and counted his passengers, making sure not to leave anyone behind.

"Please, Lord, help keep us safe," Noelle whispered. And he found himself echoing her prayer.

The driver took his seat and closed the doors. "Everyone ready?" he called out.

"Yes!" the chorus of replies rang out from the shoppers.

The driver put the bus in gear and slowly stepped on the gas, sending the bus waddling like an overweight hippo toward the exit. Caleb couldn't help glancing back at the squad car, willing the deputies not to come out too soon.

It wasn't until the bus hit the highway, kicking up speed, that he allowed himself to relax. Granted they weren't out of the woods yet, but if the drugstore clerk did recognize them, there was a good chance the deputies might check the other stores, as well. They'd been at the drugstore earlier that morning but maybe the cops would try to see if anyone remembered seeing them more recently, like early this afternoon. Thankfully they'd gotten on the bus and hadn't gone into any of the stores.

After several miles had passed and they took the on-ramp to the interstate, Caleb took a deep breath and let it out slowly. They were safe for now.

Thank You, God!

Noelle unclenched her fingers as they rode along the interstate. Close call. Too close.

She'd sensed the tension radiating off Caleb from the seat behind her and knew he'd been worried, too. But the closer they got to Madison, the better she felt. No matter how much she'd feared Caleb initially, he'd kept her and Kaitlin safe so far.

She'd prayed the whole time the cop car had been parked at the shopping mall and had to believe God was watching over them.

"I'm hungry," Kaitlin whined, interrupting her thoughts.

"We'll eat soon," Noelle reassured the little girl. "As soon as the bus drops us off, okay?"

"I wanna eat now," Kaitlin persisted. The thrill of riding the bus was fading fast.

Noelle racked her brain for a distraction. "Why don't we play the alphabet game?" she suggested. "There's a sign for Acorn Road. That's *A*. Can you find a sign with the letter *B*?" Kaitlin could only read simple sentences, but she knew her letters by heart.

The old tried but true car-ride game kept Kaitlin pre-occupied for a while, and Noelle had to smile when Caleb and some of the elderly shoppers sitting nearby joined in the game. Soon the back half of the bus was shouting out letters of the alphabet until they were stumped on the letter Z.

"There! Henry Vilas Zoo!" someone shouted.

"I didn't know there was a zoo in Madison," someone else complained.

"Let's play again!" Kaitlin yelled.

But the bus had already slowed down to pull into the parking lot of a senior-living high-rise.

"We're home," Lydia murmured. Noelle wished they really were home rather than heading to another impersonal hotel room.

Being in the back of the bus meant waiting for everyone else to get off first, before they could make their way outside. She glimpsed Caleb pressing a folded bill into the bus driver's hand as a way of saying thanks.

Her muscles were sore from all the running she'd done earlier, but she ignored the discomfort as she got off the bus and then faced Caleb. "I saw a fast-food restaurant a few blocks back," she murmured. "Kaitlin needs to eat."

"I saw it, too," he said. "Let's go."

For the first time in hours they relaxed and enjoyed a quick meal. Caleb asked one of the restaurant workers about motels nearby and thankfully, there was one just a half mile away.

Kaitlin's energy had rebounded after lunch and she skipped between them as they walked toward the hotel. There was no pool advertised but there was a nice playground, which would hopefully keep Kaitlin happy.

"Swings!" Kaitlin shouted, running toward them.

Caleb took off after his daughter. "Wait up, Katydid."

Noelle followed more slowly, smiling as Caleb pushed his daughter on the swing. Noelle dropped onto a park bench to watch, knowing Caleb deserved some time to bond with his daughter.

She could leave now, she rationalized. Kaitlin didn't seem afraid of her father anymore. Of course, that could be partially because Noelle was there with them. Would the little girl freak out if she left? There was a part of her that wanted to believe Kaitlin would.

No, she couldn't leave Kaitlin just yet. What if the little girl suffered more night terrors? A very strong possibility after they'd barely escaped the explosion. The sound of the explosion was probably all too similar to the gunshot that had taken her mother's life.

"Noelle? Is something wrong?" Caleb asked.

Since when was he so tuned in to her emotions? She forced a smile. "No, I'm fine. Just tired." Massive understatement, but complaining didn't get the job done. In fact, she and Caleb needed to talk. Maybe later, after Kaitlin fell asleep. Because Caleb needed to hear about the black truck that she'd noticed following her. And about the man she'd seen with his wife shortly before she was murdered.

No matter how painful it was for him. Although why she cared about Caleb's feelings she had no idea.

She was so far outside her comfort zone right now that she had to pinch herself to make sure this wasn't some sort of nightmare. But no, here she was, on the run with a little girl and her father, a strange man who she barely knew yet trusted to keep her safe.

"Noa, come swing wif me!" Kaitlin shouted.

Unable to say no to the child, she rose to her feet and crossed over to sit beside Kaitlin. She gave herself a small push with her foot, enough to cause her to swing back and forth in a gentle motion. She vaguely remembered swinging on the swings as a child. Some happy memories before the abuse started.

"Come on, surely you can do better than that," Caleb teased. "Hang on," he advised. She tightened her grip seconds before she felt the heat of his strong hands in the small of her back, giving her a big push.

"Higher, Noa, higher!"

Knowing Caleb would only push her again if she didn't go higher, she pumped her legs to keep up the momentum. And when Kaitlin let out a shrill laugh she found herself joining in.

Maybe she was losing her mind. How else could she explain feeling so lighthearted and happy mere hours after running for her life?

Very simply, she couldn't. And right now, she decided to enjoy the moment.

Noelle didn't say anything about the mysterious black truck that had followed her before the shooting until after they finished dinner and then put an exhausted Kaitlin down to bed shortly after eight o'clock. It was still light outside thanks to the approaching summer solstice so she pulled the heavy curtains over the window and set the air conditioner on low.

The hum of the fan provided white noise that would hopefully prevent their voices from waking up Kaitlin.

"You should try to get some sleep," Caleb said in a low voice.

"So should you." She slid into a seat next to him at the small table in the corner of the room. Their knees brushed and she swiftly moved back out of the way. "There's something you need to know, Caleb," she said, partially to distract herself from his nearness.

His gaze narrowed and he went tense. "Oh yeah?"

She licked her dry lips. "In the week prior to you getting out of jail and coming over to pick up Kaitlin, I noticed a black truck following me."

"What?" He spoke so loud she jumped in her seat. She sent a worried glance over at Kaitlin, but thankfully the girl didn't stir. He lowered his tone. "Did you call the police?"

"Actually I did, but the officer I spoke to told me I needed to get the license plate number before they could do anything." She hunched her shoulders defensively. "But that doesn't matter. The black truck must belong to the shooter. He must have been somewhere close by that day you came to pick up Kaitlin."

"Why didn't you say something before now?" he asked with a frown.

"For one thing, I wasn't entirely sure I could trust you," she admitted. Hard to believe she'd only known Caleb for roughly twenty-four hours. And even more amazing to know she learned to trust him in that same short time frame. "And after the explosion there wasn't time to talk privately."

His expression cleared. "I guess I can't blame you for not trusting me right away," he murmured. "All you had was my word that I was innocent of the crime I'd been arrested for."

She wanted to reach out to put her hand on his arm to offer comfort and had to twist her fingers together to stop herself. "It's obvious to me that someone wants to silence you and the only thing that makes sense is that the same person likely killed your wife."

For a long moment his dark gaze bored into hers. "Does that mean you believe me?"

She couldn't deny what he seemed to desperately want to hear, the reassurance that someone was on his side. Besides, the more she watched him interact with his daughter the more she knew there was no way he would have murdered his wife with Kaitlin sleeping in a bedroom nearby. And for sure, he wouldn't take off, leaving his daughter behind.

"Yes. I believe you."

He stared at her another long moment before he glanced away. "Thank you," he said in a husky tone. "Now, if I could only figure out who was driving that black truck, we'd actually have something to go on."

"I never did get the plate number. But there is something else you should know. I was working at the preschool on that Friday before your wife was killed. Earlier that day, Heather was late picking up Kaitlin."

Caleb sighed. "I was working the evening shift that day. But that sounds like her. Heather was always running late."

She leaned forward in an attempt to get him to understand. "Twenty minutes late, Caleb. And when she showed up, she wasn't alone."

He seemed to brace himself, his gaze resigned. "She was with a man, wasn't she?"

She hated being the one to tell him this, but she nodded. "Yes. It wasn't until much later, after the murder and your arrest that I realized the significance. I went to the police and told them what I saw, but without a name there wasn't much they could do."

"They didn't ask you to work with a sketch artist?" he asked incredulously.

She shook her head.

He narrowed his gaze. "Describe him for me."

It wasn't easy to go back more than a year to dredge up the memory. "He was tall, over six feet, I'd say. He had dirty-blond hair that was cut short." He stared at her so intently she sensed she was failing the description test. "He had narrow, beady eyes and was hovering at the door scowling while Heather picked up Kaitlin."

"How was he dressed? In a uniform?"

"No. Dress slacks and a blue polo shirt."

"Any tattoos? Piercings?"

Helplessly she shook her head. "Nothing that I can remember. I'm sorry, Caleb. I wish I could give you something more."

"It's not your fault," he said with a sigh. "I can't help but think he must be one of the guys from the team. I can probably eliminate a few of them based on your description but there are too many possibilities left over to start throwing around accusations. I need proof."

She couldn't bear the way Caleb sounded so dejected. At the moment they still didn't know much more than they had when this mess started.

There had to be a way to figure out the identity of the mystery man she'd seen at the preschool that evening.

The man who had likely been having an affair with Caleb's wife. And since she didn't want to believe Caleb had killed Heather, she figured a jilted lover would have just as much of a motive.

But how on earth would they be able to prove it?

SIX

Caleb stared up at the ceiling, long after Noelle had crawled into bed with Kaitlin, unable to wipe the pleased grin off his face. Noelle believed him.

She believed him!

How ironic that the person who'd known him the least amount of time was the one who stood by him now. Even his best friend hadn't done that.

Thinking of Declan made his smile fade. He wished Declan had trusted him, because he could use some help in getting to the bottom of this mess. At least Declan had dark hair. Deck couldn't possibly be the guy Noelle had seen at the day care center. Even if Deck hadn't believed in Caleb's innocence, he wasn't the type of guy to have an affair with his best friend's wife. He and Deck had often worked the same shifts anyway, and the last time they'd been together their photographs had been splashed across the front page of the newspaper after they'd rescued a child from the Underwood Creek.

That's it! He abruptly sat up. Maybe he could get Noelle to identify the man with Heather if he searched on the internet for photos of various members of the SWAT team. If they couldn't find a photo of the guy, at least they could eliminate some of the others right off the bat.

But where to find a computer? With a sigh, he stretched back out on the bed. He might have enough money to buy a tablet for computer access, but they were already running short on cash. He didn't remember seeing a computer in the hotel lobby, but there might be a small business center with a computer that they could use.

He crept out of bed, intending to go down to find out, when Kaitlin screamed. He spun around, his heart lodged in his throat at the horrible sound. He made his way over to where Noelle was holding his daughter close, trying to soothe away the night terrors.

Watching helplessly, he took a seat at the side of the bed next to Noelle, trying to be supportive as his daughter sobbed with heart-wrenching agony. Noelle murmured comforting words to Kaitlin, and soon the intensity of his daughter's crying lessened to the point they faded away.

Still, Noelle continued to hold Kaitlin close. He ached to offer his daughter comfort, too.

After what seemed like an hour, Noelle gently tucked Kaitlin beneath the covers.

"Are you okay?" he whispered.

"I'm fine. What about you?" she whispered back.

He didn't think he could ever be fine, not until his daughter's night terrors went away for good. "I hate hearing her cry like that. Do you think the explosion caused this nightmare?"

"Probably," she agreed. There was a long moment as they stared at each other in the darkness. "Try to get some sleep, Caleb, there's nothing more we can do now, okay?"

"Okay. Good night," he whispered, rising to his feet and heading over to the other bed. His previous happy mood vanished in the wake of his daughter's nightmare.

And despite his lack of faith, he found himself praying for God to bring Kaitlin the peace she deserved.

The next morning, Caleb climbed out of bed first and quickly made use of the bathroom. Shaving the stubble off his face felt great and despite the seriousness of their situation, he was anxious to get started on his investigation. The guy who murdered his wife must have targeted Caleb because he thought Caleb might figure out the truth. Which made him determined to do just that. First item on the agenda was to get downstairs to search for a computer.

When he emerged from the bathroom, he found Noelle and Kaitlin were awake now, too.

"Good morning," he greeted them.

"I'm hungry, Daddy." Kaitlin's smile didn't show any evidence of her earlier nightmare.

Just hearing her call him daddy warmed his heart. He smiled. "The hotel offers a free continental breakfast, so we can eat whenever you're ready."

"Sounds like a plan," Noelle said cheerfully. "After breakfast we can go to church. I saw one located just a few blocks down the street. Are you ready to get washed up, Kaitlin?"

Noelle grabbed clean clothes for the both of them out of the plastic bag before disappearing into the bathroom. He shouldn't have been surprised about Noelle's intent to go to church but somehow he was. He considered letting them go to the service alone, so that he could get started on the computer search. But then he remembered how he'd prayed during those long moments in the bus while watching the cops drive through the parking lot.

No, he couldn't let them go alone. Not that he'd really planned on keeping up with Noelle's Christian teachings once this nightmare was over. Surely he could hold off doing his computer search for an hour or so.

As he waited for Noelle and Kaitlin he cleaned up the hotel room, putting the dry clothes away and leaving out the ones that were still slightly damp that Noelle had set out to dry the night before. He turned on the news, anxious to hear what the media had to say, but there were only talk shows, which didn't interest him in the least.

Thirty minutes later, Noelle and Kaitlin were ready and they all headed down to the lobby for breakfast. He caught sight of a small room off to the side that housed a computer and a printer, and couldn't wait to get started.

Church first, he reminded himself. The computer would be here when they got back.

As they filled up on cold cereal, fruit and bagels he explained his plan to Noelle. "After church, I'd like you to take Kaitlin outside to play on the swing set while I search for photos of the SWAT team members. I'll save them on the hard drive and then let you review them, see if you recognize anyone." He'd thought about printing them out, but decided that it might be easier for Noelle to see the faces on the computer screen.

"All right," she agreed cautiously. "Are we checking out today? Or staying another night?"

Good question. As much as he felt the need to keep moving, the fact that this place had free breakfast and computer access made him want to stay. "Maybe we'll stay one more night," he said slowly. "By then we should have something to go on."

Noelle's expression was troubled and she looked as if she wanted to say something, but then glanced down at Kaitlin and simply nodded. "All right."

They finished the meal and then walked outside to

head down to the church. The distance was farther than he'd originally thought, and the church bells chimed as they walked up.

He felt a little bit like a fraud as he followed Noelle and Kaitlin inside. Kaitlin didn't seem upset about going to the church service so he knew that his daughter was used to accompanying Noelle.

Glancing around, he noticed that the small church was surprisingly full. When Noelle picked up the hymnal, he followed her lead.

She sang the opening hymn, her voice clear and beautiful. He didn't know the words at all, but was content enough to listen to Noelle sing. To his surprise, Kaitlin joined in, too, but only during the chorus, which was probably the only part of the song she knew by heart.

Caleb could admit that he'd planned on being bored during the service, but he wasn't. In fact, he wondered if the pastor had known exactly what he needed to hear, especially when his sermon was centered all about learning to keep God's faith and following God's plan. He'd never considered looking to God for guidance. And when the pastor read from the book of Psalms, the words reverberated through his heart and his soul.

Teach me, Lord, the way of your decree, that I may follow it to the end. Give me understanding, so that I may keep your law and obey it with all my heart (Psalms 119:33-34).

From beside him, Noelle murmured the words under her breath, as if she knew them by heart. He was ashamed that he'd never bothered to read anything from the Bible. For one thing, he'd always thought it would be dull and boring. But the passage from the Psalms was lyrical and enlightening.

What else had he missed?

The closing hymn was another upbeat song that Noelle sang along to with gusto. He found himself wishing he knew the words and the melody so he could join along. He was content, though, to listen to Noelle's and Kaitlin's voices blend together.

When the service was over, he rose to his feet and followed Noelle and Kaitlin outside, feeling lighter and filled with hope despite everything that had happened.

Was this why people went to church? Not just to pray but to hand their burdens over to God?

Maybe. If so, he figured he should attend church more often.

"Thank you for going along with us," Noelle said as they walked leisurely back to their hotel. "I think it was nice that we could share the service together with Kaitlin."

"You've taken her to church often, haven't you?" he asked, even though he already knew the answer.

"Yes." She slanted him a sidelong look. "I hope you don't expect me to apologize for it."

He had to laugh. "No, I don't expect you to apologize. I'm actually very grateful that you were there for my daughter during the months I couldn't be. And I'm glad she's learned to love God and to pray."

"You are?" Surprise echoed from her tone.

"Yes, Noelle, I am."

"Does that mean you believe in God, too?"

He pondered her question for a moment. "I think deep down I believed in the concept of God," he admitted. "But my parents didn't go to church much, so I never really gave religion much thought. Heather wasn't very religious, either, so we didn't make God or church a big part of our life."

"I guessed that Heather wasn't much of a believer," Noelle said.

He let out a soft sigh. "The demise of our marriage wasn't all her fault."

"I know. But you weren't the one who had an affair, right?"

"Right." How had they gotten on this subject? The last thing he wanted to do was to discuss his failures. He saw the park with the playground up ahead and pointed it out to Kaitlin. "Would you like to play outside for a while?" he asked.

"Yes! Can we, Noa? Can we?"

"Sure," Noelle agreed, smiling down at Kaitlin. Then she turned toward him. "Promise me that you'll let me know what you find out."

"I will. I need you to help ID this guy, remember?" They parted ways at the playground. Caleb quickened his pace to get back to the hotel's computer room. After he settled down in front of the computer, he clicked on the internet and began searching for various news stories.

Finding clear photographs of his former teammates wasn't easy, many didn't show their faces, but after an hour he had at least a half dozen, including a photo of Declan.

He stared at the picture of his best friend for a long minute. What would happen if he contacted Deck now? Would his buddy believe him? Or hang up on him?

Surprisingly, he was tempted to find out. Maybe if he was alone, he'd take the risk. But no way was he going to put Noelle or Kaitlin in danger.

With a sigh, he moved on to another search attempt, but this time, a news caption on the home page caught his eye.

Body found floating in Lake Michigan believed to

be that of Kenneth James, eyewitness to the murder of Heather O'Malley.

With a deep sense of foreboding, Caleb clicked on the headline and read the article. The body of his neighbor Kenneth James had been found almost ten days after his disappearance. And who had the most to gain by Kenneth's death?

Caleb O'Malley. After all, he was now a free man because there was no eyewitness against him.

He sat back in disbelief. Even though he'd been in jail when Ken had disappeared, the reporter believed it was possible Caleb had arranged the murder from prison.

Once again, he was a prime suspect in this latest murder investigation. And if he were arrested again, he felt certain he'd be convicted.

Noelle enjoyed being outside in the sun with Kaitlin, who'd found another little girl to play with on the swing set. Yet she couldn't help feeling like she needed to get back inside the hotel to help Caleb search for members of the SWAT team.

She glanced at her watch for the third time, and decided that an hour was plenty of time for Caleb to have found some photographs. After everything they'd been through, she found she desperately wanted to help clear his name. She needed to go in and review what he'd discovered.

"Come on, Kaitlin, it's time to go inside," she called.

"Not yet, Noa," Kaitlin protested. "We're having fun, aren't we, Izzy?"

The little blonde nodded eagerly. "Lotsa fun," Izzy said.

"Ten minutes," Noelle said firmly. "You can always come back to play later."

"But Izzy won't be here later," Kaitlin said, thrusting out her lower lip in a pout.

Noelle suppressed a sigh, and fought back a wave of impatience. There was no rush. Caleb had agreed to stay here another day. Certainly there was plenty of time to search the internet.

"Izzy," a blonde woman called out. "Time to go home. We have to get ready to go to your cousin's birthday party."

"Okay." The little girl obediently slid off the swing. "Bye, Kaitlin."

"Bye, Izzy." Kaitlin's sad eyes followed her new friend as Izzy ran over to her mother.

"Come on, Kaitlin, let's go inside for a while," she said, holding out her hand. Kaitlin reluctantly came over, her head hanging down dejectedly. Her heart squeezed in sympathy, knowing that if they were home right now, they'd be making playdates with other girls from pre-school.

She took Kaitlin into the lobby and walked over to the small computer station. Caleb glanced up at her, his expression grim. "What's wrong?" she asked.

He glanced at Kaitlin and shook his head. "I have some photos for you to look at," he said, rising to his feet so she could sit down. She noticed he had a short list of names written on a single piece of paper. "They're in order from left to right."

"All right." She clicked on the first image and couldn't help a small gasp when she realized the photograph was of Caleb and another man next to a small child who was wrapped in a blanket. "Who is this guy standing next to you?" she asked.

"Declan Shaw."

He didn't say anything more and she shook her head. "That's not him."

Caleb nodded and she saw a flash of relief in his eyes before she clicked on the next photograph. The image wasn't as clear and she stared at it for a long time before slowly shaking her head. "Nope, that's not him, either."

As she went through the next five photographs, Caleb made notes on the list. She sat back with a sigh. "None of these is the guy I saw. Maybe you're wrong about him being on the SWAT team?"

"I don't think so," he said shortly. "There are several guys whose photos I haven't been able to find yet."

"What's wrong, Caleb?" she asked, glancing over to make sure Kaitlin was still preoccupied with drawing her picture. There weren't any crayons, but Kaitlin didn't seem to mind as she used a pencil to draw a picture of a clown. "You look upset."

He hesitated, and then bent over to use the mouse to click on a newspaper article. The headline made her feel sick to her stomach.

"I don't believe it," she murmured as she scanned the article about the death of Kenneth James, the missing eyewitness from Heather O'Malley's murder investigation. "I don't understand why anyone would think this."

"I do," Caleb muttered harshly. "This is another attempt to get me convicted of murder."

The thought of someone going to such great lengths to do just that made her blood run cold. She shivered and tried to think rationally. "But, Caleb, you were obviously in jail when this happened. What possible proof could they have that you arranged this from behind bars?"

"I don't know. The only man I had regular contact with while in jail was my lawyer, Jack Owens. And he's the only one I called from the hotel where our car suddenly exploded. As much as I hate to admit it, Jack Owens is the key. Although, this new twist certainly doesn't help him any. He's being implicated in this murder investigation, too."

"That doesn't make any sense," Noelle said in a low tone. She swiveled in her seat to stare up at Caleb. "Remember what you said about someone from the SWAT team having the knowledge and ability to tap into Jack's phone? What if that same guy who murdered Heather did that and more? What if he's truly setting up both of you for this murder?"

Caleb abruptly straightened. "You could be right. I have to warn Jack."

"Wait." She caught his hand before he could leave. "How are you going to do that? If you call him they might track the call and find us. And we don't have a vehicle to drive over to find him."

"I'll take a bus," he said. "You and Kaitlin can wait here."

"No way," she protested, jumping to her feet. "What if something happens to you? We'd be stuck here without money or a way to get to safety. We're going, too."

"Too dangerous," he argued. "I'll leave you some cash. If I'm not back before nightfall you can go to the closest police station for help."

The thought of sitting here and waiting hours for him to return was excruciating. Not knowing what was going on was worse than the fear of going along with him to the place this all started. "Caleb, please. Let us go with you to the city. We'll find someplace safe to wait while you talk to Jack. Don't make us sit here in a different city, alone."

He shook his head but didn't say anything more. She

couldn't help feeling that splitting up was the worst thing they could do. But how could she convince Caleb?

Caleb knew that the best thing for Noelle and Kaitlin was to stay hidden in Madison. Yet leaving them here alone didn't sit well with him, either.

He didn't think they'd been followed here. How could they have been? They came on a bus chartered by a group of senior citizens. There was no reason to believe that Noelle and Kaitlin wouldn't be safe here. While taking them along with him would be far too risky.

They walked back to their room, a heavy silence hanging between them. He understood Noelle's frustration, but he needed to do the right thing to keep them safe. No matter how much he wanted to have their company.

"You can't stop us from buying bus tickets, too," Noelle said once they were inside the room. She stood near the doorway, with her arms crossed defensively over her chest. "We'll come along regardless."

"You don't have any money, Noelle," he reminded her.

"I'll use my credit card. I know the number by heart."

He batted down a flash of anger. "That wouldn't be smart and you know it. Whoever tried to kill me knows we're together. He'll find you in a heartbeat if you use your credit card. Don't you see? I have to warn Jack that he's at risk and I don't want you and Kaitlin in any danger. It's best for all of us if I go alone."

"Daddy?" Kaitlin came over and held her arms up. "Up!"

Flustered, he reached for his daughter, lifting her against his chest and holding her close. She'd never asked him to hold her before and he was thrilled that she was growing less afraid of him.

As if Kaitlin sensed what was going on, she placed

both of her palms on either side of his face and peered at him with a serious expression. "We go with you."

"Ah, well. I don't think so…" His voice trailed off. He could take them with him and find a hotel in Milwaukee that wouldn't be too far from Jack's house. They could stay long enough to warn his lawyer and maybe get some extra money, too. He hadn't paid for the second night yet. Why not spend one night in Milwaukee? He'd have to be close by if he intended on digging into his wife's death anyway.

"All right, we'll all go," he said with a sigh. "But we have to hurry as it's almost past checkout time."

"Thank you," Noelle murmured. Most of their things were already packed, but she quickly gathered the rest and tucked everything inside the bag.

He tried to tell himself this wasn't a mistake as they made their way down to the lobby. On one hand, it would be easier to keep both of them safe if they were close by. But the bigger reason he'd agreed was that he needed to be closer to Milwaukee in order to figure out what was going on. And that meant finding a safe place to stay in the city.

Once they'd checked out, he looked at the map and found the directions to the bus station. Their timing was almost perfect as the next bus to Milwaukee left in fifteen minutes.

The bus ride took about an hour and a half, longer than driving in a car but then again, the bus driver didn't go anywhere near the posted speed limit, which added time to the trip. When they reached the bus station and stood to get off, his gut twisted with nerves.

"Where to?" Noelle asked.

He took a deep breath and pulled himself together.

"Jack lives in a condo downtown, but there's a cheap motel nearby where we'll stay for tonight."

"All right," Noelle agreed.

They walked the two blocks to the inn and went inside. "We need a room for tonight," he said.

"Sorry, no vacancies right now, but I can put you on a waiting list in case of a cancelation."

No vacancies? He couldn't hide his surprise. "Not even one room is available?"

"Not with the Milwaukee Lakefront Marathon going on." The clerk shrugged. "Sorry."

Caleb put a fake name on the waiting list and headed outside. He wanted to get Noelle and Kaitlin someplace safe before he headed over to Jack's place. Seeing as it was Sunday, he figured the attorney would be home, rather than at his office.

"Let's just get a taxi and head over there," Noelle said. "We'll stay in the taxi and drive around the block or something while you meet with Jack."

As if on cue a taxi pulled up. "All right, get in."

The three of them slid into the backseat, Kaitlin tucked between them. Caleb gave the taxi driver the address and thanks to the marathon, they had to go the long way to get to Jack's condo.

"Wait here," he said when the taxi pulled up in front of Jack's condo.

"I keep the meter running," the taxi driver warned.

"That's fine." Going around the block wasn't an option as most of the roads were closed anyway. He went inside and buzzed Jack's doorbell.

No answer. He pushed the buzzer again. A young woman wearing shorts and a T-shirt came out through the main door. He caught the door before it closed. "I'm here to see my friend Jack," he muttered as he strode past.

The woman shrugged and continued on her way. He took the elevator up to the third floor and walked down the hall to room 303. He rapped on the door, but there was no answer. He turned to leave, but then tried the door handle just in case, surprised to find it unlocked.

"Jack?" he called, taking a hesitant step inside. "Are you home?"

A horrible smell assaulted him as he walked farther into the room, filling him with a sense of dread. He stopped short, not surprised when he saw Jack's body lying on the floor in a pool of blood.

SEVEN

Noelle tried to wait patiently while Caleb was inside talking to Jack, but it wasn't easy. She looked out the taxi window at the crowds of people walking along the street getting ready for the marathon. Useless to even attempt to look for anyone out of place.

After what seemed like an hour but was only ten minutes, Caleb came out of the condo. He paused, holding the main door open as he swept the bottom of his T-shirt along the side of the door before stepping back and letting it swing shut behind him.

His expression was tense as he jumped back into the taxi. "Please take us to the bus station," he told the driver.

Why on earth would they be going back to the bus station? "Did you see Jack?" she asked in a low tone.

Caleb's lips thinned and he scrubbed his hands wearily over his face. "I'll fill you in later," he said.

His grim tone was not at all reassuring. But of course Caleb wouldn't want to say anything in front of his daughter. And she didn't blame him, considering Kaitlin's night terrors.

"Wait, stop here," Caleb said as they passed a small park.

"Forty-five dollars," the taxi driver said, after he'd pulled over to the side of the street.

She almost choked at the high fee but Caleb handed the guy some cash and then climbed out from the taxi, pulling out their bag of belongings and then holding the door for her and Kaitlin.

"Look, Noa, a slide!" Kaitlin shouted. She took off running, heading straight toward it.

She and Caleb followed more slowly. "What happened back there, Caleb?" she asked.

He stopped about ten feet from the slide and set the bag down while watching as Kaitlin went up and down the slide with a whoop. "I found Jack dead in his condo. I'm fairly certain he was murdered."

"What?" She gaped at him in horror. Whatever she expected, it wasn't this. "How do you know?"

"The bullet hole in his gut was a good clue."

She put a hand over her mouth, trying to hold back a wave of nausea. "We have to call the police," she whispered.

"I know. But the fact that I stumbled on the body isn't going to look good for me," he said. "I tried to wipe my prints off the doorframe and the door handle, but for all I know, my prints will be found inside somewhere. After all, he was my lawyer."

And now he was dead.

She shook her head emphatically. "No one will believe you had anything to do with that."

"Do you think it's a coincidence that the body of Kenneth James conveniently showed up in Lake Michigan shortly around the time frame that Jack Owens was murdered?" he asked. "Not hardly. And you can bet Jack's death will be used as another nail in my coffin."

She didn't want to believe it, but she could see only too well how this would play out in the media. And if she hadn't gotten to know Caleb O'Malley over these past few days, the man who would do anything to make his daughter happy, the man who'd gone out of his way to protect her, she likely would have believed he'd done all these horrible deeds.

But he was innocent, of that she was sure. And not just because she secretly admired him.

"We need to do something," she said helplessly.

"Yeah, well, I'm open for ideas."

"I'm your alibi, right? We've been together since we left my house."

"Yes, I've considered that," he admitted. "But if I'm being framed, do you think the murderer hasn't already come up with some sort of plan? I'm worried your name will be dragged through the mud right along with mine."

"My name? Why?"

Caleb silently watched his daughter play for several long minutes. "Think about the night my wife was murdered. There was an eyewitness, right? Someone who must have been bribed to lie to the police. What's to prevent the real murderer from planting more lies? Lies about you and I having some sort of secret affair? Anything to discredit you as a solid alibi."

She could barely wrap her mind around what he was saying. "No one who knows me would ever believe something like that."

"Anyone will believe anything with enough evidence," he said bluntly. "Trust me, I thought the same thing once. I thought for sure proving my innocence was a slam dunk. Instead I spent over a year behind bars."

"Push me, Daddy," Kaitlin called out from the swings. "I wanna go higher!"

When Caleb went over to do as his daughter asked, she stayed where she was, his words tumbling over and over through her mind. She didn't want to believe he was right. That people would actually think the worst about her.

But she couldn't deny the horror Caleb had lived through for the past fourteen months, either. And now his lawyer was dead. Murdered. Why wouldn't the real murderer try to frame Caleb for that, too?

Caleb was right. He would be the primary suspect. And so was she, now that her name was linked to his. What could they possibly do to prove their innocence?

Noelle tried to shrug off the sense of impending doom as they spent the afternoon at the park, eating hot dogs and popcorn from a nearby sidewalk vendor for dinner. They walked a few blocks to the city bus stop and Caleb studied the map for a long moment before deciding on a route.

When the number ten bus pulled up, she was surprised to see Caleb gesture for her and Kaitlin to precede him inside. She knew that one of her preschool teachers came in from the number ten bus and the preschool center wasn't far from where she lived. Were they heading back toward the scene of the original crime? Why else would Caleb have decided to take this bus? Unless it intersected with another route that would take them far away from the city?

She was about to take a seat near the front, but Caleb urged her to head to the back.

"Where are we headed?" she asked. Kaitlin wanted the window so she let the child climb in first, before taking the aisle seat.

"I know a reasonable place to stay on the outskirts of the city," he said.

The outskirts of the city? Wasn't that area under the jurisdiction of the Milwaukee County Sheriff's Department, where his former SWAT team worked? She swiveled in her seat to face him. "Are you crazy?" she whispered. "Why would you take us back there?"

His gaze was enigmatic. "Trust me," he murmured.

She let out a sigh and tried to do that. Caleb must have some sort of plan, right? She closed her eyes and tried to pray. *Dear Lord, please guide us on Your path while keeping us safe in Your care. Amen.*

Kaitlin seemed to enjoy riding the bus although her eyelids were starting to get heavy by the time they arrived at their destination. They had to walk a few blocks, but soon they were approaching the Forty Winks Motel. Caleb requested another room with two double beds and used a story about getting mugged to avoid handing over his ID. The fact that they were there together acting the part of a family helped and the clerk accepted the cash.

"We need a plan," she said in a low voice while making sure Kaitlin was preoccupied with watching the Disney Channel.

"I know. I'm thinking of calling my buddy Declan."

She remembered the photo of Caleb and his teammate standing side by side holding a small child they'd pulled to safety from the creek. "Are you sure you can trust him?" she asked.

"No, I'm not sure of anything right now," he admitted. "But what choice do I have? We can't stay on the run forever and we're going through my cash reserves pretty quickly."

Her stomach knotted with anxiety especially knowing that this room was pricier than their previous ones. "Maybe I can pull some money out of my bank account. Wouldn't that be safer than trusting one of your former teammates?"

"And then what? We go on the run for how long?"

he asked wearily. "The cops will catch up to us eventually, especially if they put out an APB. The three of us can't hide forever. No, we need help investigating these murders."

"And you can trust this guy, Declan?"

"Deck was once my closest friend not to mention the best man at my wedding." Caleb's tortured gaze made her want to wrap her arms around him. "If I can't convince Declan that I'm innocent I won't be able to convince anyone."

She didn't know what to say to that, because she sensed he was right. "What's the plan?"

"I'd like you to stay here with Kaitlin while I try to get in touch with Declan."

Instinctively she wanted to protest, but what was the alternative? Kaitlin was already looking sleepy from all the time she spent playing outside. There was no way she could leave Kaitlin alone. And the poor child deserved at least the chance for a good night's sleep. One that hopefully wouldn't be disturbed by night terrors.

"All right," she agreed with a small sigh. "But try to hurry back, okay? I won't be able to sleep until I know you're safe."

"I'll come back as soon as possible," he promised with an intense gaze. "I'm lucky to have you."

She ducked her head, trying to hide a blush. He didn't mean it the way it sounded and she was stupid to think even for a moment that he had. "That's not exactly true. I feel like I'm holding you back."

Caleb reached out to take her hand in his, his grip radiating heat. "Noelle, you're helping me more than you realize by keeping my daughter safe. And I'm sorry I dragged you into this mess with me. If I'd known…" His voice trailed off.

"You wouldn't have done anything differently," she pointed out. "Besides, I'm convinced that God has a plan for us. We've managed to get out of tight spots before, haven't we?"

A smile tugged at the corner of his mouth and she had to resist the urge to throw herself into his arms. "A few weeks ago I might have scoffed at that notion, but now I'm beginning to think you may be right."

His admission warmed her heart. "I'll pray for your safety and for Declan to believe in you."

"I'll gladly take all the help I can get." His fingers tightened briefly around hers before he released her and rose to his feet. "Don't answer the door to anyone but me, okay?"

"I won't."

He glanced back at Kaitlin once more as if debating whether to go and give her a hug and a kiss. But he didn't, maybe because Kaitlin was curled up in the bed, hugging her Giffy, her eyes at half-mast. She knew it wouldn't be long before Kaitlin was sound asleep and Caleb must have known it, too.

He pocketed one of the room keys and opened the door.

"Be safe," she whispered. He nodded and then slipped outside before she could say anything more.

After making sure the door was secure, she climbed into the bed beside Kaitlin and settled in to wait.

Please, Lord, keep Caleb safe in Your care.

Leaving Noelle and Kaitlin was more difficult than he'd anticipated, but he tried not to dwell on it as he silently jogged through the streets of Wauwatosa. He took a zigzag route, more to keep away from prying eyes than any fear of being followed.

He didn't have much of a plan, other than trying to catch up with Deck at his home. If his buddy was working, he'd be forced to wait until the end of his shift.

As he made his way to the familiar neighborhood of Declan's place, he mentally went through a few scenarios in his mind, trying to think of a way to convince Deck he was innocent. That is, if Deck even gave him a chance to say anything at all.

He shoved aside the depressing thought and slowed down to a walk as he approached Declan's modest house.

Darkness hadn't fallen yet so he couldn't be sure that Deck was actually home. But then he caught sight of a bluish glow from the television in the living room. Even from this distance he could tell Declan was watching a baseball game.

For a moment he battled a wave of regret, wishing for simpler times when watching a baseball game was commonplace instead of being completely outside the realm of possibilities. He felt conspicuous as he stood for a moment, trying to garner the courage to face his friend.

A car drove by, spurring him into action. He went up the driveway, bypassing the front of the house to knock at the side door. It took a minute for his buddy to respond and when Declan finally opened the door, the expression of pure shock on his face made his heart sink a bit.

"Hi, Deck, do you have a minute? I need a friend."

Declan's mouth opened and then closed again without a word. Caleb was afraid Deck was going to shut the door in his face, but then he pushed it open and stepped back, allowing him room to come in.

"Thanks," Caleb said. "I know you probably believe the worst, but I swear I'm innocent. I didn't kill Heather and I certainly didn't kill anyone else, either."

Declan stared at him for a long moment. "Give me one reason I should believe you."

Fair enough. "Because you know how much I love my daughter, Kaitlin, and you know I'd never kill my wife and then leave Kaitlin there alone with her dead mother."

Declan pursed his lips for a moment and then shrugged. "I never could figure out why you'd kill Heather," he finally admitted. "But when Ken James came forward stating he saw you, I figured you must have snapped or something."

"I didn't snap. I was framed."

Declan sighed and stared up at the ceiling for a long moment. "Why do I get the feeling I'm not going to like your theory?"

Relieved that Declan hadn't booted him outside, he chuckled. "Because you're a smart man, that's why."

"You'd better come in, then," Declan said, gesturing toward the living room. "The Brewers are losing anyway."

Caleb hovered in the doorway. "I'd rather we talked somewhere private so that no one can see me," he said. "For your own safety more than mine."

"My safety?" Declan scoffed. "I'm not the one accused of murder." Despite the comment Deck walked through the living room to pick up the TV remote. He shut it off and then turned back to face Caleb. "Do you want to sit here or in the kitchen?"

"Kitchen." Caleb wanted to be far away from the front living room window where anyone walking by could see inside. Declan's kitchen overlooked the backyard, which in turn butted up against his neighbor's backyard. Caleb took a seat at the table and tried to gather his thoughts.

Deck pulled two water bottles out of the fridge and

handed one to Caleb. "Start at the beginning," he suggested.

Declan knew about the very beginning, his being arrested for Heather's murder, so Caleb started with getting out of jail and heading over to pick up his daughter from Noelle's house. Declan didn't say a word throughout the entire dissertation until he got to the part where he went inside Jack's condo to find him dead.

"Whoa, whoa, back up. Are you serious? Your lawyer was murdered?"

Caleb battled a wave of defeat. If Deck didn't believe him he was sunk. "Yes, he died from what looked to be a slug in the gut. And you can bet that my fingerprints will be conveniently found at the scene of the crime."

"Wow." Declan took a long gulp of his water. "I don't know anyone who hates you that much."

A flash of anger bubbled up before he could stop it. "Why in the world would I make all this up, Deck? And who said it's about hating me? What if this guy is just going to great lengths to hide his tracks? I have to believe he's running scared, otherwise why would he risk leaving a trail of dead bodies in his wake?"

"You have a point," Declan grudgingly admitted. "But, Caleb, you have to admit this is a whopper of a story. I mean, seriously, even Hollywood couldn't come up with a plot this convoluted."

His shoulders slumped and he dropped his head in his hands. "I know I'm asking a lot," he said in a low voice. Caleb forced himself to meet Deck's skeptical gaze. "But if you don't want to believe this guy is going to extreme measures to set me up, then give me something. Tell me what motive I have for risking my freedom by killing Jack. Especially now when I've finally been released from jail."

Declan slowly shook his head. "There is the possibility that you used Jack to arrange for Ken's murder. That Jack was going to rat you out so you killed him, too."

Hope deflated in his chest like a popped balloon. *This is it,* Caleb thought. *This is when Deck will throw me out of his house without offering any help.*

"Who am I kidding?" Deck abruptly said, throwing up his hands in defeat. "No way am I buying that story. For one thing, it doesn't even make sense. Why would Jack help you commit murder, for Pete's sake, and then suddenly get cold feet and threaten to turn you in? Why even risk his law license in the first place? No, you're right. This whole thing reeks of a setup."

The wave of relief was so overwhelming that it took several seconds for Deck's words to sink in.

"Really?" Caleb asked in a hoarse voice. "You really believe me?"

"Yeah, I believe you." Deck held up his fist so Caleb could bump knuckles with him. "I should have gone with my gut all along," Declan continued. "You're not the type to resort to violence."

Thank You, Lord!

First Noelle and now Declan. He didn't think it was a coincidence that he managed to get two people on his side. Maybe this was God's will.

"You have no idea what your support means to me," Caleb finally managed. To have Noelle's support was one thing, but to have his best friend back was even better. "I feel like I've been fighting alone for so long."

"Well, you're not alone any longer," Deck said with a grim smile. "So tell me, what can I do to help?"

Caleb swallowed hard. "I need assistance with investigating Heather's murder. And I need more cash. You know I'm good for it, Deck, or I wouldn't ask."

"I'm fine with lending you cash, but what's the point of investigating your wife's murder? If the scene was staged to frame you, there's no point. The clues are already tainted."

"Yeah, but consider this—Noelle saw Heather with a man the night she was murdered," he reminded Deck. "That's a place to start."

"Maybe," Declan said as he looked away.

The hairs on the back of his neck lifted in warning. "What?" he demanded. "What do you know about Heather?"

Declan winced, and shook his head. "Nothing you need to know."

"Deck, you have to tell me. If it could have anything at all to do with Heather's murder, then you have to tell me!"

Declan let out a heavy sigh. "I'm sorry, Caleb. But Heather was seeing more than one guy. From what I heard she was stringing several guys along."

Several? Caleb felt sick as he searched Declan's gaze, trying to figure out if his buddy was lying to him.

Because if Deck wasn't lying, and his wife really had been seeing multiple men, then they were no closer to finding out who'd framed him for Heather's murder.

EIGHT

Noelle was too wired to fall asleep. Images of Caleb's dead lawyer lying on the floor bleeding kept flashing through her mind and she feared this time she was the one who'd suffer a night terror instead of Kaitlin.

When there was a soft rap on the door, she literally shot to her feet, her heart thundering in her chest. Using the peephole she verified that it was Caleb standing there before she unlatched the dead bolt and opened the door.

She tensed when she realized Caleb wasn't alone, although it didn't take long for her to recognize that the man standing next to him was the same guy from the photograph in the newspaper. The one where they'd rescued a small child.

"Grab your key and come outside for a moment," Caleb whispered.

She did as he requested, staying near the closed door so that she'd be sure to hear Kaitlin if the little girl woke up crying. "What's going on?" she asked.

"Noelle, this is Declan Shaw," Caleb said, glancing up and down the front of the motel, and she knew by now he was trying to make sure there wasn't anyone listening to their conversation. "Deck, this is Noelle Whitman.

She's Kaitlin's preschool teacher and was my daughter's temporary guardian, too."

"Nice to meet you, Declan," Noelle said in a polite tone. "Does this mean you finally believe Caleb's innocence?"

Deck lifted an eyebrow. "Wow, she doesn't pull any punches, does she?"

Caleb grinned, looking younger and more relaxed than she could ever remember seeing him look before. "Noelle has been a huge help to me. I wouldn't even be here now if it wasn't for her."

Being reminded of everything they'd been through over the past few days sparked a rare surge of anger. "And why wouldn't you have stood by your best friend through all this anyway?" she demanded in a low, fierce tone, glaring at Declan. "Caleb shouldn't have had to go through this alone."

"Easy, Noelle, it's not all his fault," Caleb murmured, putting a hand on her arm.

"No, she's right, Caleb. I deserve her anger." Declan's gaze was contrite when he looked at her. "I'm sorry. I should have stuck by Caleb, and probably would have if there wasn't an eyewitness who vowed he saw Caleb shoot Heather. Not that it's a good excuse, but since I knew about his wife's affairs, I figured it wasn't a stretch that he might have snapped."

"By affairs, you mean more than one?" She couldn't believe what she was hearing. Could this situation get any worse?

"Yeah, unfortunately, that puts a crimp in our theory that the guy you saw with Heather that night was actually the one who may have killed her," Caleb said. "For all we know that guy she was with wasn't anyone from the SWAT team."

She leaned back against the door, battling a wave of helplessness. "But you were so convinced that someone from the SWAT team set you up. And what about having the resources to find my car even after you swapped the license plates? Who else could do something like that?"

"We'll figure it out. Don't worry," Caleb said reassuringly. "We're not alone anymore. Deck is going to help us. In fact, he's allowing us to borrow his laptop."

She wished she could be as hopeful as Caleb seemed to be now that they had Declan's support. But she couldn't quite shake a sense of unease. It felt like they were taking several steps backward for every inch they moved forward.

"You really think someone from the team set you up?" Declan asked.

"Yeah, I do." Caleb lifted his chin. "Obviously someone knew enough about police work to plant evidence and bribe an eyewitness. Someone who knew I might not be arrested unless there was an eyewitness."

Declan raked his hands through his hair. "Marc Brickner."

"You actually saw Heather and Marc together?" Caleb asked.

"Only once," Declan confirmed. "But now that you mention suspecting someone from the team, Marc was pretty vocal about believing you were guilty. He kept going on and on about what a horrible husband you were to Heather. And about your out-of-control temper."

"I need to find a picture of him for Noelle," Caleb muttered.

"Here, I'll find one." Declan used his smartphone to search the internet and then handed the device over to Noelle. "Is this the same guy you saw with Heather?" he asked.

She stared at the photo on the screen, feeling a bit light-headed to have finally put a name with the face. She slowly nodded. "Yes, that's him."

"Well, that gives us a place to start," Caleb said.

"Yeah, especially since Brickner was seen with Heather the night she was murdered," Declan agreed.

Noelle couldn't seem to tear her gaze from the photo on Declan's phone. Somehow she thought she'd feel relieved once they knew exactly who was behind all of this.

But she didn't. Instead her sense of foreboding only deepened. Because, somehow, she knew that identifying this man was only the beginning. And she feared Caleb might end up like Jack Owens.

Dead.

Miraculously, Kaitlin slept through the night without waking up once. Noelle wished she could say the same. But when she heard Caleb get up and head into the bathroom, she rubbed her gritty eyes and swung up to a sitting position at the side of the bed she shared with Kaitlin.

Caleb had left Declan's computer on the desk, so she turned it on and quickly found the motel's free wireless network. She did a quick search on Marc Brickner and found several more photos of him. He looked different wearing all his SWAT gear, but there was no mistaking that he was the same man who'd been with Heather that Friday night she was twenty minutes late to pick up Kaitlin.

The guy never seemed to smile. In each and every photograph his mouth was compressed in a thin line. Compared to the photograph of Caleb and Declan smiling and holding the young child they'd rescued, this Marc guy looked like he was capable of doing illegal activities.

But did that include killing his teammate's wife? His mistress?

Maybe. Yet even she knew they needed some sort of motive.

She typed Heather's name into the search engine, and immediately several photographs popped up on the screen. Caleb's wife had truly been a beautiful woman, at least on the outside.

"Noa?" Kaitlin called and she quickly shut the top of the computer down, so that the young girl wouldn't see the photographs of her mother.

"Good morning, Kaitlin," she said, getting up from the desk. "Did you sleep well?"

"Yes, but I hav'ta go to the bathroom."

As if on cue the door opened and Caleb came out, fully dressed with the only evidence of his shower being the drops of water glistening on his hair. "The bathroom's all yours, ladies," he said cheerfully.

Kaitlin scampered inside but Noelle didn't immediately follow. Instead she went back over to the computer, opened it up and disconnected from the internet.

"Find anything?" Caleb asked.

"Not really. I just wanted to be certain that Marc Brickner was really the man I saw with Heather."

"You already knew that, didn't you?"

She suppressed a sigh. "Yes, but I felt the need to be sure, in case I made a mistake." She paused and then added, "I can't explain it, but I'm scared, Caleb. I'm afraid that, somehow, he's going to find us before we find him."

Caleb lifted his hand and lightly cupped her cheek. "I'll protect you and Kaitlin with my life if necessary, Noelle. I will do everything possible to keep you both safe."

She leaned into his hand for a moment, wishing he'd

take her into his arms and hold her. She could use a bit
of his strength.

"Noa, are you coming?" Kaitlin asked from the bathroom, breaking the moment.

"Yes, I'm coming." She reluctantly drew away from
Caleb, hoping he wouldn't notice her pink cheeks. Why
was she longing to be close to Caleb? She'd made up her
mind to avoid relationships, because she didn't trust a
man not to hurt her.

But, unfortunately, she trusted Caleb.

She picked up the bag of clothes and ducked into the
bathroom to shower and change, reminding herself that
Caleb wasn't the type of guy to be interested in someone plain like her. After all, his wife had been a beautiful model.

With her chaotic feelings firmly in check, she and
Kaitlin finished getting washed up. When they emerged
from the bathroom about twenty minutes later, she was
surprised to find that Caleb had breakfast spread out on
the small table in the corner of the room.

"Where did you get all this?" she asked.

"Deck brought us breakfast," he said with a wry grin.
"I think you made him feel guilty last night and he's trying to make amends."

"He should feel guilty," she muttered. She couldn't
help her spurt of anger at the man who'd claimed to be
Caleb's best friend. The aroma of scrambled eggs and
bacon made her mouth water, distracting her.

"Yay, bacon!" Kaitlin exclaimed, climbing up onto
one of the chairs.

"Hold on, we have to pray first, remember?" Noelle
said.

Kaitlin sat back on her heels and put her hands together. Caleb mimicked his daughter's movements.

She took a deep breath and let it out slowly, gathering her thoughts. "Dear Lord, we thank You for providing this food for us to eat and for bringing us the help we need to clear Caleb's name. And we ask You to guide us on Your chosen path. Amen."

"Amen," Caleb and Kaitlin said simultaneously.

They enjoyed the meal, and while she wanted to grill Caleb about where Declan was now, she didn't want to say too much in front of Kaitlin. When they finished eating, she cleaned up the mess while Caleb packed their things. Kaitlin was glued once again to the Disney Channel.

"I take it we're moving on?" she asked, trying not to be too depressed about going to yet another impersonal motel room. Who would have thought that being on the run was so incredibly wearying?

"Deck thought we might be better off staying at his place for a while," Caleb said. "He has two spare bedrooms and we wouldn't have to use up our cash."

Ridiculous to feel annoyed because Caleb made arrangements with Declan without asking for her input. She should be glad that they had someone helping them. That Caleb had someone else who actually believed in him.

There was a soft knock at the door. Caleb peered through the peephole before allowing his buddy to come in.

"We have a problem," Declan said, his expression grim.

"What?" Caleb asked.

"There's been a warrant issued for your arrest related to the murder of Jack Owens."

Caleb shouldn't have been shocked at the news, but there was no denying that he felt as if someone socked him in the solar plexus. "Brickner must be the driving force behind that," he muttered.

"Now what?" Noelle asked helplessly.

He didn't have a good answer. He turned back toward his daughter. "Kaitlin? Do you remember Uncle Declan?"

Kaitlin ducked her head shyly and he realized that in the year he'd been gone, Kaitlin's life had been turned totally upside down. Was it any wonder she didn't remember everything from their former life together? Especially since she'd likely blocked a lot of the horror from her mind?

"Hi, Kaitlin," Declan said with a broad smile. "You've grown up a lot since the last time I saw you."

Kaitlin ran over to Noelle as if seeking support. Noelle pulled her close in a reassuring hug.

"Uncle Declan is a friend of your daddy's," Noelle said softly. "There's no reason to be afraid."

Caleb turned toward Deck. "So what do you think we should do? I don't blame you if you've decided against hiding a fugitive in your home."

"Don't worry about me. There's no reason for anyone to suspect that after all this time, I've decided to help you out," Declan said thoughtfully. "But we need to make sure that no one sees you going inside my place."

Caleb wished he'd gone to Declan's last night, but even when his buddy had suggested it, he hadn't wanted to wake up Kaitlin. The last thing he'd wanted was to cause another night terror for his daughter. He should have factored in the possibility of having a warrant out for his arrest.

"I guess I could ask the hotel if we can stay another night," he said, trying to hide his reluctance.

"I was thinking more along the lines of sneaking you

in the back of my car," Deck said with a frown. "I think the sooner we get you hidden inside my place, the better."

"But it's broad daylight," Noelle protested.

"I know, but I made sure I wasn't followed here," Declan said. "And my place has an attached garage so if you hide on the floor, no one will be able to see you. Especially if you stay hidden on the floor until we're safely inside the garage."

"Let's go, then," Caleb said, anxious to get moving. He couldn't help feeling as if the minute anyone saw his face they'd start shouting for the police to arrest him.

"I'm parked right in front of the motel," Declan assured him. "And I'm ready if you are."

Noelle looked worried, but she gathered up the bag when he lifted Kaitlin in his arms. Moving swiftly, they slipped outside and headed for Declan's SUV.

He gestured for Noelle to get in the front seat. She put the bag on the seat and then crouched down on the floor of the car, keeping her head low and using the plastic bag for additional cover. He was impressed because he couldn't see her unless he was right next to the passenger door.

"We're going to play a hide-and-seek game, Katydid," he said as he set his daughter down in the back. "Can you crouch down on the floor of the car like this?" He demonstrated what he wanted his daughter to do.

"You're too big to fit, Daddy." She giggled as she crouched down behind the driver's seat. "I'm a better hider."

"That you are," Caleb agreed.

As soon as they were safely inside, Declan put the car in gear and backed out of the parking lot. Caleb didn't like the fact that he couldn't see where they were going, but he knew he had to trust Declan.

His life, as well as Noelle's and Kaitlin's, depended on it.

For a moment he wondered if he should turn himself in to the police. Declan would be able to keep Noelle and Kaitlin safe, and maybe playing by the rules would work for him instead of against him.

But as soon as the thought formed, he rejected it. Too much had happened to turn himself in now. Especially since he didn't know how much evidence they'd fabricated against him.

The car swayed as Deck took several twists and turns, no doubt taking the extra-long way home.

"I don't wanna play this game anymore, Daddy," Kaitlin whined. "I want to sit up on the seat."

"Not yet, let's just stay down here a little longer, okay?" He reached over to take his daughter's hand, willing her to stay put. He didn't want to have to hold her down there against her will.

"We're almost there," Declan called from the front seat.

A few minutes later, Caleb heard the garage door going up. "There, see?" he said to Kaitlin. "Very soon we'll be able to get out."

"Is there a swing set?" Kaitlin asked.

He fought a wave of guilt. "I don't think so," he said.

Kaitlin thrust out her lower lip. "A swimming pool?"

"No, I'm afraid not." He wanted to give his daughter something to look forward to, but Declan was a bachelor and likely didn't have any toys lying around.

"I don't wanna stay here." Kaitlin pouted. "I wanna go back to the motel."

Declan pulled into the garage and they stayed where they were until the garage door shut behind them.

No one spoke until they were inside the house. The

minute the door closed behind them, Declan turned toward Kaitlin. "Would you like to play with a dollhouse, Kaitlin?"

Caleb gaped at his friend. "Why on earth do you have a dollhouse?"

"I have twin nieces that I babysit for once in a while," Delcan said with a shrug. "I found out that having a dollhouse made for much nicer visits, at least for me."

"Yes! I wanna see the dollhouse!" Kaitlin literally danced from one foot to the other. "Where is it, Unca Deck! Where's the dollhouse?"

"In the spare bedroom. Come on, I'll show you." Declan took Kaitlin by the hand and took her upstairs.

"I bet she'd go with a stranger if they held out a dollhouse," Caleb said darkly as he followed Kaitlin's departure.

"I don't think so," Noelle said. "I think deep down she remembers Declan, the same way she remembered you. Besides, we're lucky Declan has nieces or this little adventure would be much worse."

That much was true. He'd panicked when Kaitlin asked for a swing set and a swimming pool. He could only hope the dollhouse would keep her occupied at least for a while.

"We'll need to stay away from the living room window," he said, trying to think through their plan. "And once the sun goes down, we'll have to remember not to put on any lights. We absolutely have to make sure that it looks as if Declan is living here alone."

"I understand." Noelle glanced around the small kitchen. "At least we can cook our meals rather than wasting our money on fast food."

"Yeah, but right now, I'd like to see the news." There

was a small radio under the counter. "Or at least listen to it."

He fiddled with the dial, finding the sports station easy enough, but that wasn't what he needed. He turned the dial again until he finally found a talk show. Noelle sat down and he took the chair across from her.

Declan came back into the room and joined them at the table. "We have to talk while Kaitlin is occupied upstairs."

Caleb stood and turned down the volume on the radio. "What happened?"

"When I heard the APB put out for you, I asked a few questions. They found Jack's body and your fingerprints were at the scene of the crime."

Caleb curled his fingers into helpless fists. "So what? He was my lawyer. How big of a stretch is it to believe I was at his house at some point in time?"

"On the murder weapon?" Declan asked.

The murder weapon? He thought back, trying to imagine the crime scene. There was a lot of blood and the awful smell. He didn't remember seeing a weapon, but then again, he hadn't searched the place looking for it, either. He shook his head. "So where was the gun found?"

Declan frowned, his gaze narrowing with suspicion. "How did you know Owens was killed with a gun?"

For a moment he stared at his friend in horror. What was going on? Did Deck really suspect him after all?

Had he brought Noelle and Kaitlin here for safety, only to be turned in to the authorities by the man he'd once believed was his best friend?

NINE

"Because he saw the bullet wound, that's how!" Noelle shouted, jumping to her feet and glaring at Declan. She wanted to smack him for being so suspicious. "What are you saying? That you really believe Caleb is capable of cold-blooded murder?"

"I didn't say that…" Declan started but she wasn't in the mood to listen.

"How dare you bring us here as if you're willing to help, only to accuse him of killing his lawyer. Are the police on their way here right now? Is that what this is about?" Noelle was so mad her entire body was trembling and she barely registered the fact that Caleb had risen to his feet and put a reassuring arm around her waist.

"Calm down!" Declan said, holding up his hands as if he might need to defend himself. "I never accused Caleb of anything. I just thought it was odd that he knew about the gun."

"Noelle is only stating what I already thought," Caleb said reasonably. "And she's right about one thing. This isn't going to work without trust."

"Okay, okay." Declan jammed his fingers through his hair and sat back in his seat with a frustrated sigh. "I'm sorry. You're right. I shouldn't have sounded as if

I believed that you had anything to do with murdering Owens. I know you wouldn't do that, Caleb. I just…lost my head for a moment."

Caleb's arm around her waist proved to be a distraction, helped ground her so that her anger faded as quickly as it had ignited. She wanted so badly to lean on Caleb but this wasn't the time to show any weakness.

Could they really afford to trust Declan?

"Apology accepted," Caleb said, giving her a slight squeeze. "Right, Noelle?"

"I don't know," she muttered half under her breath. She allowed herself to lean against Caleb at least a little. "Maybe."

Caleb brushed a soft kiss against her temple and for a moment she forgot Declan was even there. She hadn't let any man get close to her for so long. Why did being with Caleb feel so right? She knew logically she should move away, but she couldn't bring herself to do it.

"Thanks for sticking up for me," he whispered.

She couldn't help but smile. "You're welcome."

Declan cleared his throat loudly and when she glanced over at him, she thought there was a flash of envy in his gaze. "I hate to interrupt, but we need to get to work if we're going to make any headway in this investigation."

Reluctantly she moved away from Caleb, missing his warmth as she dropped back onto the chair she'd vacated. Every one of her senses was tuned in to Caleb as he sat beside her.

"I'm listening," Caleb said.

"As I was saying, the murder weapon was found in the Dumpster outside the condo with your fingerprints on the handle of the gun."

Noelle rolled her eyes. "I'm not a cop and even I think that's ridiculous. Why would an experienced former

SWAT team member be so stupid as to leave the gun right outside the scene of the crime?"

"Yeah, I hear you, but obviously someone believes it or there wouldn't be a warrant out for Caleb's arrest," Declan said dryly.

"Any idea who found the body?" Caleb asked. He reached over to take her hand in his, once again distracting her from the conversation. She didn't know why he kept touching her, and she sternly told herself not to read too much into his small, subconscious gestures.

"A neighbor reported a bad smell coming from Jack's condo. The Milwaukee police went in and found him."

"So now the MPD is working with the sheriff's department?" Caleb mused.

Declan snorted. "Yeah, not likely. You can be sure the sheriff will take over the case from MPD."

"And Sheriff Cramer never liked me much," Caleb said with a sigh. "I shouldn't be surprised at the way he chose to believe the worst."

"Cramer doesn't like me, either," Declan pointed out. "Don't read too much into that. It's likely Captain Royce fed him an earful about you. Remember how he called us hotshots after we rescued that kid? As if we did that just for the media exposure? The guy's a jerk."

Noelle frowned. "So what do Sheriff Cramer and Captain Royce think about your buddy Marc Brickner?" Noelle asked, dragging her attention back to the conversation.

The two men exchanged a knowing glance and she knew that couldn't be good.

"Well?" she demanded.

"Brickner is Royce's protégé," Caleb admitted. "And since Royce was promoted by Sheriff Cramer, it's likely they both think Brickner is the best guy on the team."

"Great. Just great." Could the scenario get any worse? "Any chance that Sheriff Cramer knew about Brickner's affair with Heather?" she asked.

Caleb shrugged. "No way to tell, but even if he did know about it, I don't think Cramer would suspect Brickner of murder."

Of course he wouldn't. That would be too easy. She glanced between the two men. "So what's our next step? Where do we go from here?"

"Maybe we should try to follow Brickner during his off-duty time, see what he's up to?" Declan suggested. "He's not scheduled to work tonight."

"We'd only find something if Brickner is doing his own dirty work, which right now, isn't a good assumption," Caleb said. "Why would he do anything suspicious now? There's a warrant out for my arrest. You can bet he'll sit back and wait for the system to work."

The thought was far too depressing. "What if Heather was involved in something illegal?" she asked.

Both Caleb and Declan stared at her as if she'd lost her marbles.

"What makes you think that?" Declan asked.

"Look, everything started with Heather's murder, right?" Both men nodded in agreement. "What's the motive? Jealousy? It seems like this cover-up is a bit extreme for something so simple."

"Heather was a model," Caleb protested. "Hardly illegal."

"Or maybe her modeling was a cover for something else," Declan mused. "Noelle could be on to something. We have to consider all angles."

Caleb removed his hand from hers and she knew that she'd upset him. She sent him an imploring look, understanding where he was coming from. It was one thing to know your wife was having an affair, or even more than one affair. But to think that the mother of your child was involved in something illegal was entirely different. Especially since Caleb was a cop, sworn to uphold the law.

She didn't blame him for not wanting to assume the worst about his deceased wife.

Caleb stared at Declan, trying to fight the natural instinct to defend Heather. If he were honest, he would admit that what Declan and Noelle were suggesting wasn't outside the realm of possibility. "She did bring in a lot of money," Caleb finally said. "But what kind of illegal activity could she have been involved with? Drugs?"

And then it hit him. What else would explain why she was seen with more than one man?

"Prostitution?" He forced the horrible word past his constricted throat.

"We don't have to jump to conclusions," Noelle interjected, looking distressed. "Drugs could be the answer."

He shook his head, appreciating the fact that Noelle cared enough to try and spare his feelings. "I think there would have been some evidence if this was about drugs. Her autopsy showed she was clean. The D.A.'s office used the fact that she wasn't drugged as evidence that she likely knew her murderer."

"So what? That doesn't mean she wasn't some sort of drug runner," Noelle repeated stubbornly.

"Heather was far too noticeable to be a mule," Declan said. "She attracted attention everywhere she went."

"There's no point in speculating." Caleb glanced at his friend. "We could spend hours going through different scenarios, but without proof we're stuck. Deck, is there anything else you can tell me from the police report of Heather's murder?"

"No, there wasn't much evidence at the crime scene," Declan mused. "The eyewitness testimony played a big role in your arrest."

No kidding. "No murder weapon was ever found?" he pressed.

"Nope." Deck shook his head. "They had nothing else to use to pin it on you."

"Interesting, considering the gun used to kill Jack was found nearby," Caleb murmured. "Why didn't they use a similar ruse back then for Heather's murder?"

"Good question," Deck admitted. "Maybe it was a crime of passion, that whoever killed her didn't really plan it. And when he did, it was too late to plant the gun."

He had to admit, Deck's theory made sense. Ironic that Brickner had spouted off about Caleb's temper when Brickner's was far worse. He could easily imagine Brickner losing control and killing Heather in a fit of rage.

Too bad he needed a way to prove it. "Could I borrow your computer for a while?" he asked Deck.

"Sure." If Deck was curious as to what he was searching for, he didn't let on. Declan pulled the laptop out of its case and handed it over to Caleb. "Do you need any help?"

"No, just give me some time, okay?" He didn't want Declan or Noelle, for that matter, to watch over his shoulder. "Would you mind checking on Kaitlin?" he asked.

Noelle hesitated, but then nodded. "Sure."

Caleb waited until both Deck and Noelle left the kitchen, before he began his search. There was something niggling at him from the back of his mind. A website that he'd stumbled across by accident, shortly before he'd moved out of the house. At the time he hadn't thought much about it.

He tried several different combinations of words before he found what he was looking for.

Eileen's Elite Escort Services.

Caleb closed his eyes for a moment, dreading what he
was about to find. But hiding from the truth wasn't going
to help him clear his name. So he took a deep breath and
entered the website, which required the viewers to be
eighteen in order to move through the various screens.
The meager attempt to prevent minors from going in
was laughable.

It didn't take him long to find Heather's photograph,
although he was a bit surprised that it was still on the
site, considering she'd died fourteen months ago. Maybe
they kept it for marketing reasons? She was beautiful,
dressed in a sexy, scanty outfit that made him feel sick
to his stomach. And he found it interesting to note that
the name under her photograph was Hannah, not Heather.

A fake name? Why not?

He closed the laptop with a wave of disgust. His wife
had been a paid escort. And what exactly did her services
entail? He wasn't so sure he wanted to know. Considering
the types of photographs he saw, he imagined the worst.

The only good thing to come out of this latest clue
that he could see was that it was another possible motive for her murder.

Caleb didn't tell Declan or Noelle what he'd found, at
least not right away. Partially because he was humiliated.

But more so because the site was probably just another dead end. Other than giving a clue as to another
potential motive for murder, what could they do with
the information?

While Noelle made lunch, Kaitlin chattered on and
on about the dollhouse and the various dress-up dolls

she'd found. He was grateful Deck had something to keep Kaitlin entertained.

"When do you work next?" he asked Deck.

Declan carried his dirty dishes over to the sink, glancing at Caleb over his shoulder. "Tonight, second shift, which means I have to leave a couple of hours. The three of you will need to keep a low profile."

"Understood. We'll make sure that we don't use any lights while you're gone and will keep our movements to a minimum." After the past few days, he couldn't deny the fact they could all use some decent sleep.

Declan scrubbed his chin. "I was thinking about that. There's only one small window in the basement, and we could board that up if you wanted to keep working on the computer. We could even move the dollhouse and the television down there, too. You could do whatever you want without anybody knowing that you're here."

"That would be great," he agreed. "We could even bring the mattress down from one of the beds."

"Let's do it," Declan said, setting his glass down with a thud. "Before I leave."

Eager to have something constructive to do, Noelle and Kaitlin carried the dolls and other toys that Declan had upstairs in the spare bedroom down to the basement while he and Deck hauled the heavy stuff. Once they had the mattresses and television strategically set up next to an old card table he planned to use as a desk, he stepped back and surveyed their work with satisfaction.

The television was small, but it was better to use the old one than to take the big screen from the living room, just in case the absence was noticed. Declan brought a few more chairs out for them to use, and Noelle dusted them off while Caleb looked around for something to use to black out the small window.

Duct tape and cardboard should do the trick. Although he was a little worried the light might shine through the cardboard. He dug around until he found a can of black spray paint. Perfect. He used the edge of the can to break a corner of the window, so that having it covered up looked reasonable, and within minutes had the window effectively blacked out.

"Nice," Deck said. "Now you guys should be totally safe down here."

"I hope so." Caleb didn't want to take any chances, especially not with Noelle or Kaitlin.

But he wanted very much to get outside the confines of Declan's house, to do a little research of his own, once Noelle and Kaitlin were asleep.

Noelle kept herself busy cleaning dust off the card table and chairs the guys had dragged out for them to use. She told herself that staying in a dark basement with only a few lights on was better than being on the run, but so far she was having trouble believing it. She kept feeling as if there were spiders crawling up her arms.

Maybe because she'd killed at least a half dozen so far.

Ridiculous to get worked up over a few spiders, but everyone had a weakness and creepy-crawlies just happened to be hers.

The time seemed to move by with excruciating slowness once Declan had left for work. She played a game of Go Fish with Kaitlin while Caleb surfed the internet on Declan's computer.

At six, she slipped back upstairs to rummage for something they could eat for dinner. She decided to make a frozen pizza, since that would be easy to carry downstairs. While the oven was preheating she found paper plates and napkins and took those back down to the basement.

Caleb had put aside the computer to play a card game with Kaitlin. She was pleased at how comfortable the little girl was around him now, compared to their first meeting outside her house.

Before the bullets started flying.

She shivered at the memory. Hard to believe that just a few days had passed since then when it seemed like a lifetime.

They ate the pepperoni pizza in the basement, and both Caleb and his daughter prayed with her before digging into the meal. Afterward, they played several more card games, which only served to make Noelle wonder what it would be like if the three of them really were a family.

Don't go there, she warned herself. They wouldn't be together for very long, just until they cleared Caleb's name.

She pushed the depressing thought aside to concentrate on the game. After they'd each won several rounds, Caleb announced it was bedtime.

Kaitlin protested, but Noelle understood what Caleb was thinking. They needed to take advantage of the ability to get some rest while they had it. Even though they were safe for now, she couldn't shake the feeling that their peace was short-lived.

Caleb turned out the two small lamps they were using and instantly the basement was plunged into total darkness.

"I don't like it so dark," Kaitlin whined.

"Is this better?" Caleb turned on the smaller of the lamps and carried it off to the farthest corner of the basement, tucking it behind some boxes to help dim the light.

"Much better, Daddy."

Sleep didn't come easy, despite the comfy mattress she shared with Kaitlin. She prayed for guidance and safety, which helped her relax. She was just beginning to doze off when she heard the soft brush of fabric and the almost imperceptible thud of a footstep.

Her eyes shot open and she turned her head in time to see Caleb heading upstairs. She almost called out to him, but held back so that she wouldn't wake up Kaitlin.

Where was he going? She rolled off the edge of the mattress, moving as silently as possible. They'd been sleeping fully dressed so all she needed to do was to pull on her running shoes before following Caleb up the stairs.

She didn't know how Caleb managed to be so silent, because the wood stairs creaked as she climbed them. She wasn't surprised to find Caleb waiting for her in the kitchen.

"Go back downstairs," he whispered when she reached the doorway.

"Not until you tell me where you're going." She heard him sigh.

"I'm just going to look around for a bit, that's all. Nothing for you to worry about."

"Why would you take that risk?" she asked, trying not to show her frustration. "Especially when there's a warrant out for your arrest? All it would take is for one person to recognize you."

"I'm just going to see if Brickner's home, that's all. I'll be back in an hour or so."

"You were the one who said that following Brickner wasn't going to do any good. So why go out now?"

Caleb's expression wasn't easy to read in the dark.

"Stay here with Kaitlin, okay? I promise I'll be back soon."

"Wait," she said, grasping his arm. "What kind of car does Brickner drive?"

"I'm not sure. I never paid attention since we didn't hang out together."

"If you're going to head over there, see if he's driving a black extended cab pickup truck."

Caleb paused for a moment and then scowled. "Just like the one that was following you in the days prior to my release."

"Yes." She didn't want him to go, but sensed there was nothing she could say or do to make him change his mind. "That might give us a hint of something to go on."

"Sounds like a plan." Before she could say anything more, Caleb slipped out the garage door, closing it softly behind him.

She stayed in the kitchen, looking out the window at the backyard, where she assumed he'd go rather than heading out front. But even though she watched intently, she never saw any sign of Caleb.

Which should have reassured her. But she couldn't suppress a shiver and rubbed her hands over her arms for warmth.

Please, Lord, watch over Caleb. Keep him safe.

TEN

Caleb slipped through Deck's backyard, taking care to stay hidden in the shadows. He didn't rush, but chose his path carefully. As much as he'd tried to reassure Noelle that he would be fine, the last thing he wanted to do was to be identified by some nosy neighbor and sent back to jail.

If that happened, he felt certain he'd never get out. Ever.

He headed for the running/biking trail and increased his pace to an easy jog for roughly two miles before veering off onto the side street that would take him past Brickner's house.

Caleb had only been there once about two and a half years ago, shortly after Brickner's divorce was final. Marc had thrown a huge Super Bowl party to celebrate his new single status. All the guys from the SWAT team were invited, so Caleb had tagged along with Declan and another buddy, Isaac Morrison. Caleb remembered the night clearly because Brickner had been a bit of a jerk, bragging about how he'd taken the house from his ex-wife. Caleb remembered thinking at the time it was a good thing Brickner didn't have any kids. The game had been boring, and Brickner had started drinking heavily, so he, Deck and Isaac ended up leaving at halftime. Now that Caleb thought about that night, he couldn't help wondering if Brickner had been having an affair with Heather even back then? And if so, what on earth had his wife seen in the guy?

Steering away from those thoughts, because really what difference did any of that make now, Caleb concentrated instead on walking past Brickner's house, trying to appear casual and not overly interested in his surroundings. From the corner of his eye, he could see there were no obvious lights on, at least none that were visible from the street.

At the next intersection, he purposefully turned the corner in the opposite direction and headed down several streets before he backtracked to the row of houses that were located directly behind Brickner's place. From this side, he could make out a small light that was on over what appeared to be the kitchen area.

One small light didn't mean much. Brickner could easily be home or out somewhere, so Caleb checked over his shoulder to make sure no one was watching before he slipped between two houses with dark windows and no sign of anyone being home to sneak up to Brickner's place.

He prayed he wouldn't be arrested for being a Peeping Tom as he flattened himself against Brickner's house and peered in through the lighted window.

He didn't see anyone, so he made his way around to a couple of the other darkened windows, hiding behind trees or bushes if any cars came down the street. When he rounded the corner of the garage, he glanced in the window and verified the garage was empty.

He hunkered down to wait a bit, even though logically he knew that if Brickner was working, the guy wouldn't be home for a good hour yet, since the second-shift guys worked until eleven-thirty at night. And if Brickner wasn't working, he likely would be out even later.

After about thirty minutes, Caleb decided to head back to Declan's place when headlights pierced the darkness. He kept hidden as the vehicle came closer, slowed down and then turned into the driveway. The garage door opened and with the light on, he could easily identify the make and model of Brickner's vehicle.

Noelle's guess had been dead-on. Marc Brickner drove a black extended cab pickup truck. He memorized the license plate, even though he vaguely remembered Noelle stating she'd never gotten the tag number.

He waited for what seemed like a long time but was only thirty minutes, when Brickner came back out, dressed in a very sharp suit, a white shirt and a tie. Not at all the usual garb worn by the guys on the SWAT team. Where was Brickner headed? Who was he meeting with? The questions barely formed in his mind when Brickner backed down the driveway and left, heading east.

Leaving Caleb to wish he had a set of wheels to follow him.

Caleb returned to Declan's house a while later, not a bit surprised to find Noelle up and waiting for him.

"You were gone a long time," she accused, meeting him once again in the kitchen. She hadn't turned any lights on, but his eyes were so accustomed to the darkness he could see her fairly well.

"I'm sorry, but Brickner came home so I hung around longer than I intended." He reached into the cupboard for a glass and poured a large glass of water to soothe his parched throat. "You were right, though. Brickner drives a black extended cab pickup truck."

Noelle's sour mood evaporated. "That's great news. Surely that helps our case."

He didn't want to burst her bubble but he also didn't want to give her false hope, either. "He's not the only guy driving a black extended cab pickup truck. We'll need more than that coincidence to convince the authorities that I'm not the killer."

"I know, but he's the same guy I saw with Heather the night of her murder. All we need to know is a little more about what was going on between them. It has to be drugs. Nothing else makes sense."

He wasn't convinced, but filled her in on the way Marc was dressed when he'd left the house. "Brickner was either meeting a woman or a boss of some sort. No one dresses like that without a good reason."

"Too bad you couldn't follow him," she murmured.

"Maybe next time," he said. He caught sight of the flash of headlights outside, so he drew Noelle into an alcove so they couldn't be seen. The peach scent of her shampoo was distracting, although he tried to keep his gaze focused on the living room window.

The vehicle outside slowed and very nearly stopped directly in front of Declan's house before it picked up speed and drove away.

"I thought for sure the car meant Declan was home," Noelle whispered close to his ear.

"No, but it was another dark-colored pickup truck," he said grimly. He released her and took a step away to put some badly needed distance between them.

She sucked in a harsh breath. "Brickner?"

"Maybe." He wished he could have gotten a good look at the driver, but that was impossible with the glare of the headlights. His gut knotted with tension at the realization. "Or there's some other guy with a dark pickup truck involved in this case. The same guy who was following you. Someone that isn't Brickner."

He didn't even want to consider the possibility that they were on the wrong track. That Brickner wasn't the one who'd murdered Heather after all.

Because without a hint of a clue, the case of his wife's murder was dead in the water.

Noelle huddled next to Kaitlin on the mattress, her mind too busy to sleep. What if Caleb was right about the black extended cab pickup truck? What if they couldn't figure out who was behind these murders?

They couldn't hide out in Declan's basement forever. She knew they were already putting Declan in a bad situation by staying here in the first place. If anyone found out he was hiding a fugitive, he'd lose his job and face being arrested, too.

She imagined Marc Brickner dressed in a suit and tie, heading off to—where? A date? Or an illegal business meeting? She supposed there was a chance he was headed to a legal business meeting, but somehow she didn't think that was likely.

The garage door opened, signaling that Declan was home. She heard Caleb get up and head up the stairs to meet his friend. Unwilling to be left out, she followed.

"We had a hostage situation," Declan was saying as she reached the top of the stairs. "I stayed late to help cover because we were a man short."

"How did it end?" Caleb asked.

"Our perp surrendered without harming his wife and kids," Declan said. "But it was touch and go there for a bit."

"Who was the negotiator?" Caleb asked.

"Isaac Morrison," Declan said, glancing over at her as she entered the room. "You'll be interested to know that Brickner was originally supposed to work tonight, but he called in sick."

"Sick?" Caleb echoed. "Well, that's funny, since I saw him leaving his house about ninety minutes ago, dressed in a suit and tie. He certainly didn't look sick to me."

Noelle was relieved at the news. "We are on the right track. I knew he was the one who was following me."

"We still don't know that for sure," Caleb protested and she understood he was trying to keep an open mind. From spending just these few days with Caleb, she was already getting a sense of the type of cop he'd been before this happened. Good cops always kept their minds open to other possibilities, a trait she couldn't fault him for. Too bad the guys who'd arrested him hadn't given him the benefit of the doubt. "Besides, it doesn't make sense that Brickner would drive past Deck's house on a night he knew Deck was likely working."

Declan straightened away from where he'd been leaning against the counter. "Brickner came here?" he asked in shock.

"A black extended cab pickup truck slowed down in front of the house and then drove away," Caleb corrected. "And really it wasn't easy to see in the darkness, for all I know it could have been dark gray or a dark blue in color rather than black."

Declan was silent for a moment. "Brickner may not have looked at the schedule, or he knew I was working and was making sure there was no one here."

"Like us," Noelle said softly.

"Yeah," Declan admitted slowly. "Maybe. Brickner knew Caleb and I were friends."

"Do you think he's been swinging by here on a regular basis?" Caleb asked.

"I don't know," Declan said in a frustrated tone. "I haven't been paying that much attention to the traffic on my street. This is a normal, safe neighborhood. The only thing I know for sure is no one has been following me."

"Did you happen to notice when Brickner is scheduled to be off again?" Noelle asked.

"Yeah, he's off the next two days in a row."

"Good," Caleb said with satisfaction. "That means we can follow him tomorrow night."

"If he goes someplace," Declan agreed.

Noelle sighed, knowing that she would be expected to stay here with Kaitlin while they followed Brickner. Not that she minded taking care of Kaitlin, but the thought of being left here in the basement without any way of knowing if they were okay filled her with dread.

She'd just have to put Caleb's and Declan's fates in God's hands.

The next morning, Noelle's eyes were gritty from lack of sleep. She dragged herself out of bed to take care of Kaitlin and within minutes Caleb was up, too. She took Kaitlin upstairs to use the bathroom facilities while Caleb straightened up their temporary living space. She brought cold cereal and milk down for breakfast and this time Caleb led the prayer.

"Dear Lord, thank You for providing this food we are about to eat and keep us safe in Your care. Amen."

"Amen," she and Kaitlin echoed simultaneously, which made Kaitlin giggle.

The thought of spending the entire day in the basement did not fill Noelle with enthusiasm. She understood the need to be safe, but it was barely an hour and she already missed having natural sunlight.

Caleb must have understood her feelings, because he gestured to the staircase with his spoon. "I think we are probably okay to head upstairs for a while after breakfast, as long as we stay out of the living room. With the bright sunlight outside, it won't be easy for anyone to see inside unless they come right up to the windows."

"That would be great," she said thankfully.

Noelle managed to keep busy throughout the next few hours, doing dishes and playing dolls with Kaitlin. When she heard Declan and Caleb talking in low tones, she left Kaitlin to her dollhouse and went down into the basement to see what was going on.

Caleb's expression was grim as he stared at the computer. She nearly gasped out loud when she recognized the photograph of Heather, Caleb's wife, on the screen. The woman was dressed in a racy outfit that barely covered the essentials.

"Where did you find it?" she asked. She couldn't imagine what he must be thinking about seeing his wife dressed like that.

Caleb and Declan exchanged a long glance. "Eileen's Elite Escort Services dot com," Caleb admitted.

"Escort services?" Noelle frowned, not exactly sure what that meant. "What exactly does an escort do?"

Caleb shook his head. "I'm not sure I want to know."

Declan's expression was equally sober. "In theory the escorts are available for wealthy men who want a good-looking woman to appear at functions with them. However, we suspect there is far more to the escort's duties than that."

She remembered what Caleb had said yesterday, about prostitution. She hadn't wanted to believe the worst, wanting to spare him the pain and humiliation. But obviously now that they found Heather's photo on this website, there was no denying the truth.

"But why would Heather's photograph still be on this site if she's been dead for over a year?" she asked.

"That's a good point," Caleb admitted. He refused to meet her gaze and she worried that he somehow felt responsible for what his former wife had done. "Either the owners aren't good at updating their website or they chose to keep the photo there for advertising purposes."

"At least we know that this is another possible motive for murder," Declan said.

"Is there a way to find out who owns this business?" Noelle asked as Caleb minimized the site as if to hide the photograph of his dead wife. She wanted to reassure him that this wasn't his fault, but considering the stiff set to his shoulders and the way he was avoiding her gaze, she didn't get the sense he would accept anything remotely resembling sympathy.

"I bet Brickner's involved somehow," Caleb muttered harshly. "The way he was dressed last night was far from subtle."

"He could be the middle man," Declan agreed. "Maybe he was reporting to his higher-ups about the business?"

Noelle wasn't a police officer but what Caleb and Declan were proposing made sense. "We need to find a way to prove he's involved." Then another idea occurred to her. "What if Heather wasn't murdered out of jealousy or rage, but because she wanted out? Maybe she threatened to go to the authorities if they didn't let her go, so Brickner killed her?"

Caleb spun around in his chair to face her for the first time since she'd come downstairs. "You could be right about that. As Kaitlin was getting older and starting school, she may have had second thoughts about being involved in this escort business."

The frank hope in Caleb's eyes tugged at her heart. She just couldn't imagine what it must be like to realize you've been betrayed to this extent by the woman you promised to love and cherish. Any illegal activity was bad enough, considering Caleb was a sheriff's deputy, but an escort service that potentially doubled as a high-class call girl? She could barely wrap her mind around the concept.

"I'm sure you're right," she agreed softly.

"Hopefully we'll find something tonight," Declan said as he moved across the room. "I'm heading to the grocery store, and will be back in about an hour."

When she and Caleb were alone, she placed a reassuring hand on his shoulder. "I'm sorry you have to go through this," she said.

His mouth thinned and he looked exceptionally weary as he shrugged. "I knew our marriage was falling apart, but I can't help thinking I should have done more. Tried harder. Figured out that something like this was going on sooner."

"Caleb, beating yourself up like this isn't going to change anything. Besides, Heather is responsible for her own behavior," she said.

He hung his head and took a long, shuddering breath. "I didn't love her the way I should have," he said in a voice so low she could barely hear him.

She put her arm around his shoulders and gave him a hug. "Maybe not, but she must not have loved you the way she should have, either."

"You're probably right about that," he admitted. "We were young and I was infatuated with how beautiful she was. I remember thinking I was such a lucky guy to have a woman like her. But after we got married and Heather discovered she was pregnant, everything changed. Heather became obsessed with her looks, with her weight. She only gained fifteen pounds with Kaitlin and she worked out like a maniac afterward." He paused and then continued, "And when Kaitlin was barely a year old she began her modeling career again. Which I'm sure was a big, fat lie."

"We don't know for sure that Heather wasn't modeling back then," she pointed out. "Maybe it was only later that she went into the escort business."

"Maybe." He shrugged. "The timing doesn't matter, so I need to just let it go."

"Your daughter needs you, Caleb. Have you noticed that she's not afraid of you anymore? Heather betrayed you and your wedding vows, but your goal right now is to clear your name so that you and Kaitlin can become a family again."

"Thank you," he murmured. She stepped back so that he could stand up, but she wasn't prepared when he gently cupped her face in his hands and stared down at her intently. "Noelle, I don't know what I would have done without you," he said mere seconds before he gently kissed her.

ELEVEN

Caleb's heart pounded in his chest as Noelle returned his kiss with a sweetness he craved. It seemed like a lifetime since he'd held a woman, especially someone as pure and good as Noelle. But their brief moment of togetherness was interrupted when Kaitlin began to wail.

"Noa! My tummy hurts!"

Noelle broke away from Caleb and he wished the lighting in the basement was better so he could search her expression. Was she upset with him for overstepping his bounds? He hadn't intended to kiss her, but then again, he couldn't deny that he wanted to kiss her again.

"I better go check on Kaitlin," she murmured, running a hand through her hair.

"We'll both go," he said, determined to take an active role in raising his daughter. If he could clear his name, or rather *when* he cleared his name, he had every intention of being a good father to his daughter.

Noelle cuddled Kaitlin close, pressing a kiss to his daughter's forehead. "She feels a bit warm."

"What should we do?" he asked. "Take her in to the doctor's office?"

"I don't think we need to panic yet. She isn't throwing up or anything. We'll just have to keep an eye on her. I'll make something light for lunch, like soup and toast."

"Cin'mon toast," Kaitlin corrected. "I like cin'mon toast."

"All right, we'll see if Uncle Declan has cinnamon for your toast," Noelle agreed.

Caleb stood there for a moment, feeling stupid. How was it that he hadn't known that his daughter liked cinnamon toast? And what else didn't he know? What else had he missed?

Too much. He realized now he should have stayed more involved in raising Kaitlin, especially after Heather returned to her so-called modeling career. He was ashamed to admit that he'd resented Heather for always getting a babysitter, when he never considered cutting back his own hours.

For a moment he wondered if spending fourteen months in jail and almost losing his daughter was God's way of sending him a wake-up call.

And if so, he was grateful for being given a second chance.

The rest of the day seemed to crawl by in slow motion, and Caleb wasn't sure if it was because Kaitlin was more fretful than usual or if he was just anxious to be doing something active to clear his name.

He spent time on Deck's computer, trying to search for more information on Eileen's Elite Escort Services, but every avenue he'd tried resulted in a dead end. He finally gave up, realizing that he and Declan would just have to put their energies into following Brickner and finding leads that way.

He played card games with Kaitlin, giving Noelle a break from the uncharacteristically clingy child. He knew Kaitlin wasn't feeling well when she only ate half of her cinnamon toast and chicken noodle soup.

Declan brought home more than just groceries, he'd purchased three prepaid phones and used a fake email address to activate them.

"Thank you," Noelle said, taking her phone gratefully. "At least now I have a way of getting in touch with you guys if needed."

"These are mostly to be used in an emergency," Deck cautioned.

"I know."

Caleb cleared his throat. "I'd like to go back to Noelle's house, see if we can figure out where the shooter was located."

"I'm not sure if that's a good idea, especially now that your mug shot has been splashed all over the news," Deck said.

"I know, but hear me out for a minute. If you and I dress in our uniforms, then no one will question us. We'll look like a couple of cops gathering clues."

"Yeah, except that the police have already done that." Deck did not look enthusiastic about his plan.

"Who are the best sharpshooters on the team?" Caleb asked.

"You were one of the best," Declan admitted. "But now Marc Brickner has the top slot."

"I just want to take a look at the trajectory," Caleb said, trying to find a way to change Deck's mind. "I think there are only a few guys who could have made that shot."

"Come on, Caleb, anyone from the team could have attempted the shot. Obviously, they missed."

"The miss was sheer luck," Caleb said. Although now that he'd learned a bit about prayer, he couldn't help wondering if maybe God had spared him for a reason. "I bent over to pick up Kaitlin's stuffed giraffe. If I hadn't, I'm pretty sure I'd be dead."

Deck seemed to consider that information before he reluctantly nodded. "All right, but I don't think going into your old house to get a uniform is very smart. I'm sure there are hidden cameras set up to monitor the place."

Caleb knew Declan was right. "I'll borrow one of yours. We're not that different in size."

"All right," Deck reluctantly agreed.

As Caleb dressed in one of Declan's spare uniforms, he realized that he'd lost weight in prison. Where once Deck's uniform might have been a bit snug, it now hung loosely on his frame.

"I need to hit the gym," he muttered in disgust as he tightened the belt.

He checked on Noelle and Kaitlin before leaving, and Noelle's eyebrows shot up in surprise when she saw him. "Wow, you look great in uniform," she said.

He knew better than to be pleased by how she'd noticed, especially since there was no guarantee that he'd be offered another job with the SWAT team even if he managed to clear his name.

Although he secretly hoped Sheriff Cramer would hire him back.

One step at a time, he reminded himself sternly. He followed Deck out to the garage, and hid down in the seat as Declan backed out of the driveway and headed out of the subdivision.

He stayed hidden for at least ten minutes while Deck drove around making sure that he wasn't followed. Deck was in his private vehicle and not a squad car, but hopefully the neighbors would assume it was an unmarked vehicle.

"You can sit up now," Declan said after he made another right-handed turn. "We'll be at Noelle's house in about five minutes."

Caleb couldn't deny he was nervous about doing this, but he really needed to see the scene to be sure that he understood the facts. So far, they were building a case against Brickner, although it was circumstantial at best. Proving that Brickner had made the shot that nearly killed him wouldn't be easy, but as a former sharp-shooter himself, he knew that the crime scene could reveal a lot about the shooter.

He climbed out of the passenger side of Declan's vehicle, trying to look as if he belonged. His beat-up red truck was gone, obviously it had likely been towed and swept over by the crime scene techs.

Had they planted more evidence to make him look guilty? He didn't want to know.

As they approached Noelle's house, he noticed that someone had nailed up a board over the broken window of her living room. At least someone had tried to protect her house from vandalism.

"Here are the bullet holes," Declan said, waving a hand at Noelle's front door. Caleb examined the one along the doorframe first, and if he stood straight the bullet hole was just below eye level.

"Thinks he's hot stuff to attempt a head shot," Caleb grumbled. Every cop knew that head shots were not usually attempted because of the small area. Chest and abdomen shots were the preferred target range.

It would be just like Brickner, a man with an overly healthy ego, to attempt a head shot.

Caleb slid a straw into the hole to figure out the track of the bullet. Turning, he carefully swept his gaze across the street. Where had the shooter been?

Then he saw the large tree between two houses, with thick branches low enough to grab onto. "How much do you bet he was up in that tree?" he asked Declan.

"Let's go check it out."

Caleb followed Declan across the street, hoping that no one was looking at him too closely. It was the middle of the day in summer and there was one elderly man mowing the lawn on a riding mower and a few doors down there were a handful of kids playing tag.

"Give me a leg up," he said to Declan.

His buddy didn't argue. With a leg up it was easier to get up into the tree, although he imagined that Brickner had managed the feat on his own.

He found the shooter's spot without too much difficulty. There was a large branch with another branch shooting off to the right, making the perfect prop for a long-range rifle. There was a small opening between the leaves through which he could see Noelle's front door.

Caleb took his time, finding the small section of the branch where the bark was worn away, likely from the weight of the rifle. He took a picture with the cell phone.

How long had the shooter sat up here waiting for his target? Several hours? Seemed unlikely in broad daylight. Even though there was an abundance of green leaves, anyone living in one of these two houses would have noticed a guy hiding in the tree.

"I bet he had an accomplice," Caleb muttered. Someone who'd tailed him from the time Caleb had left the jail? Possibly.

He swung down from the tree and dropped to the grass beside Declan. As they left the scene and walked back to Declan's vehicle, he grew more certain that the shots were fired by Brickner.

But who was Brickner's accomplice?

* * *

Caleb was relieved when they returned to Declan's house without catching anyone's attention. He swept his arm across his sweat-dampened brow, thinking that being a criminal wasn't easy. All this skulking around, trying to hide from view? And for what? A little extra cash?

"How's Kaitlin?" he asked when he saw Noelle cleaning up the lunch dishes in the kitchen.

"She says her tummy hurts, but so far she seems okay. I found a thermometer in Declan's medicine cabinet and she has a very low-grade fever. Nothing to worry about yet."

He didn't like the thought of Kaitlin being sick. "We could send Declan out for medicine to help bring down her fever," he offered.

"That would probably be a good idea, just in case her fever spikes later tonight." The pucker between her brows was an indication of her worry. "And for sure if we have the medicine we won't need it," she added with a wry smile.

He wanted to pull her close and hug her, but he held back, unsure what she thought about their kiss earlier. He told himself not to push his luck. "Why don't you make a list of things you think we might need?"

"Good idea."

He changed his clothes while Noelle wrote out her list. He hung up Deck's uniform with a pang of envy. He told himself that a career didn't make the man, but he was too afraid that in his case it did.

What would he do for work if he couldn't get hired back on the SWAT team? He might be able to find a security job somewhere, maybe at one of the local hospitals. The idea didn't hold a lot of appeal, but he needed to remember that his daughter was his first priority.

Everything else was second.

After Declan returned from the local pharmacy with the items on Noelle's list, he took a tray of cheeseburgers outside to place on the grill. When Caleb protested, Deck insisted that he grilled for himself often and that no one would think it was suspicious that he was grilling so many.

Kaitlin didn't eat much, but Caleb hoped her appetite would return tomorrow. He and Noelle figured Kaitlin had caught some sort of twenty-four-hour virus.

When dinner was over, he and Declan cleaned up so that Noelle could play another card game with Kaitlin. Even though it was still light outside, he and Declan planned to leave soon, unwilling to take the chance that Brickner might slip away before they arrived.

"Call if you need something," Caleb said to Noelle as she and Kaitlin played a game of Go Fish on the mattress they used as a bed in the basement.

"Declan was pretty clear that I can only use the phone in case of an emergency."

"Yeah, well, I'd appreciate a text message so that I know Kaitlin is okay."

She smiled as if pleased that he cared enough to ask about his daughter. "All right, I'll text you."

"Good." He wished he had the right to kiss Noelle goodbye, but he had to be satisfied with getting a big hug and a kiss from his daughter.

"I love you, Daddy."

"I love you, too, Katydid." When he glanced at Noelle he thought he saw the gleam of tears in her eyes. "Stay safe," he murmured before heading upstairs to find Declan.

They parked the next block over and used Declan's binoculars to keep an eye on Brickner's house. As the sun disappeared behind the horizon, Brickner left the house in his shiny black pickup truck.

"We've got him," Caleb said to Declan. "He's heading east on Palmer."

His buddy drove around the block, keeping a decent amount of distance behind Brickner's truck. Declan followed him all the way out to what looked to be a gentleman's club, but Brickner surprised him by not going inside. Instead he parked in a corner of the lot that was farthest away from the light.

A small blue car drove up, and headed directly over to where Brickner's truck was. Using the binoculars, Caleb watched Brickner get out of the truck and meet the woman who was dressed much like the photograph he'd seen of Heather. Not the same clothes of course, but just as revealing.

"Write down this tag number," he said to Declan and rattled off the license plate for the blue car.

"A hot date?" Declan asked.

"I don't think so," Caleb murmured. "She's yelling at him about something. I can't read her lips, but he's yelling back at her. Wait, now he's hauling her into his truck!"

"Let me see," Declan demanded. "Is he actually kidnapping her?"

"Not exactly. She's sitting with her arms folded over her chest and gazing out the passenger window as if resigned to her fate." He handed the binoculars over to Declan. "We need to follow them."

Declan took a quick look before handing them back to Caleb. Deck started the car. "I think we're in for a long night."

Caleb kept the binoculars trained on the reluctant passenger in Brickner's truck for as long as he could, silently agreeing with his buddy's assessment of the situation.

He hoped and prayed they'd uncover something to crack the case wide open. Because he didn't want to let down Noelle.

Or his daughter.

Noelle didn't remember falling asleep, the bone-deep exhaustion from the night before must have caught up to her. But when Kaitlin began to cry, she jerked awake. "What is it, Kaitlin? What's wrong?"

"My tummy hurts," Kaitlin whimpered. Noelle had a bad feeling and barely made it out of the way before Kaitlin threw up all over.

"Oh, sweetie," she murmured, grabbing the edge of the blanket and using it to wipe the mess. "Come on, we need to get upstairs to the bathroom."

She had her phone in her pocket, but she couldn't call Caleb, yet. She carried Kaitlin upstairs and this time managed to make it to the bathroom so that the little girl could be sick in the toilet.

"I don't feel good, Noa," Kaitlin whined.

"I'm sorry, honey. Here, let me wash you up." When she reached for the washcloth and towel hanging on the rack, she belatedly remembered to close the bathroom door so that the light wouldn't be as noticeable to anyone outside.

Although there wasn't much she could do about the small bathroom window, other than making sure the blinds were closed.

After a few minutes, Kaitlin seemed to be better, although Noelle knew that was likely temporary. She left Kaitlin in the bathroom for a few minutes while she went out and found new sheets and blankets for the mattress downstairs.

She didn't want to waste too much time, so she balled up all the soiled stuff and carried everything over to the washer and dryer. Once she had one load of wash in, she remade the bed, sprayed a liberal dose of air freshener and went back upstairs to get Kaitlin.

"I'm hungry," Kaitlin announced.

"We'll try some crackers and white soda first," Noelle told her. Kaitlin followed her into the kitchen, where Noelle found a can of white soda and a package of saltine crackers. Then she emptied out a wastebasket to use as a bucket.

"I wanna sit at the table," Kaitlin insisted, crawling up onto a chair.

Noelle hesitated, glancing fearfully outside. The backyard was completely dark, and the kitchen was tucked away toward the back of the house. If they kept only the bathroom light on, they might be okay there for a few minutes.

Kaitlin sipped the white soda and nibbled on a cracker. Noelle prayed the child's stomach would tolerate the light fare. She texted Caleb about how Kaitlin got sick, and frowned when she didn't get a response.

She hoped the lack of response meant that Caleb and Declan were busy following Marc Brickner. The sooner they found some evidence against the guy, the better.

A flash of headlights pierced the darkness and she leaped up to flip off the switch for the bathroom light, plunging the room in darkness.

"Noa? I'm scared," Kaitlin whispered.

"I'm here, sweetie, don't worry." It wasn't easy for her eyes to adjust to the lack of light, but she felt along the wall until she found Kaitlin. "We're going to go back downstairs, okay?"

"Okay," Kaitlin agreed.

Noelle handed Kaitlin the crackers and then lifted the child into her arms while balancing the can of white soda. She carefully descended the basement steps, leaning heavily on the rail while her heart pounded erratically against her ribs.

She breathed a tiny sigh of relief when she reached the bottom. The light was on over the washer, so she was able to move quickly now, setting Kaitlin on the mattress and then dousing the lights.

Inexplicably paranoid, she turned off the washing machine and strained to listen. For several long moments she didn't hear anything except Kaitlin munching a cracker.

Just when she'd convinced herself she was making a big deal about nothing, she heard the distinct thud of a footstep above them.

Someone was inside the house!

TWELVE

Caleb's attention was focused on the road Deck was following toward some sort of old, nondescript garage-type building. He could see Brickner's black extended cab truck parked along the side, partially hidden beneath an overhang of trees.

"I think this must be their headquarters or something," Declan was saying as he parked along the side of the road, refusing to go too close. "Let's go check it out."

Caleb's phone vibrated with an incoming text message, and he frowned as he read the message. Declan opened the car door, intending to get out, but Caleb clamped his hand on Deck's arm to hold him in place.

"Wait," Caleb said. He read the message twice to make sure he was seeing it correctly. "Noelle's in trouble. She thinks someone is in your house."

"What?" Declan stared at him in disbelief. "How is that possible?"

Caleb was busy texting a reply. Stay hidden in the basement.

We are now, but Kaitlin threw up so we were up in the bathroom with the lights on. Someone could have seen us.

Caleb's stomach clenched with fear at the news. Having the flu was bad enough for Kaitlin to suffer, but this was worse. If Brickner had assigned someone to watch over Declan's place, they'd know Noelle and Kaitlin were there. He quickly relayed the information to his buddy. "We have to go back, Deck. Now."

Declan didn't hesitate, but closed his car door and swung the vehicle around in a sharp U-turn in order to head back the way they'd come. Declan pushed the speed limit as much as he dared, but Caleb knew they were a good fifteen to twenty minutes away. He texted Noelle. We're coming.

Hurry.

They were hurrying, but clearly she was afraid. He could almost taste her fear. Feeling helpless, he closed his eyes and prayed.

Dear Lord, please keep Noelle and Kaitlin safe in Your care. Please!

Noelle desperately searched the basement for something to use as a weapon. There was a fishing pole, too flimsy. Several previously opened cans of paint, useless. Finally she saw a couple of cans of wasp spray and figured one of those was better than nothing.

After tucking the canister under her arm, she wrapped Kaitlin in a blanket and carried her to the darkest corner of the basement. They huddled on the cold cement floor, partially hidden behind some boxes. Unfortunately, there weren't too many places to hide within the basement, and no time to clean up the evidence that they'd been living down there. The mattress on the floor, the laptop computer set up on the card table and the chairs set up around it would give away the truth.

She gripped the can of wasp spray in her right hand, and held Kaitlin close with the other. Up above, the footsteps on the floor seemed incredibly loud as the intruder moved from room to room, as if he was making no attempt to be quiet. Because he knew they were trapped with nowhere to go? The only way out was up the stairs. She tightened her grip on the wasp spray, trying to gather her courage.

"I'm scared," Kaitlin whispered.

"Shh," Noelle said, pressing the little girl's face closer to her neck to help muffle the noise. "We have to be quiet until your daddy gets here."

Kaitlin nodded, seemingly reassured to know that Caleb was coming home. Noelle swallowed hard, hoping Caleb and Declan would arrive soon. She wanted to believe the men would get there before the intruder found them. And she hoped and prayed that Kaitlin wouldn't throw up again.

The seconds ticked by with excruciating slowness. The footsteps stopped and she breathed a sigh of relief.

But then she heard the door open at the top of the basement stairs and the *thunk, thunk, thunk* as someone came down the steps.

She shrank against the boxes as much as possible, hardly daring to breathe. The intruder must have flipped on the overhead switch because the area suddenly flooded with light and she could easily make out the huge, hulking body of a man holding a gun as he stood sweeping his gaze around the basement. At the moment his back was to them, but for how long?

"You can't hide from me," he said in a harsh, raspy

voice, making her cringe with fear. "Come out now and no one will get hurt."

Noelle's mouth was so dry she couldn't have made a sound if she wanted to. Not that she believed him anyway. He had a gun, certainly he intended to hurt them or at the very least, take them away. But why? She had no clue.

And other than the wasp spray there wasn't much she could use to defend herself and Kaitlin. Even if she tried to make a run for it, she'd have to carry Kaitlin, which would slow her down even if she could outrun the guy, which she didn't think was remotely possible.

It struck her in that moment that she may have to give up her life in order to save Caleb's daughter. And she silently prayed to God for strength and for protection.

The man moved away toward the opposite end of the basement. But her relief was short-lived as he quickly made his way around the room until he was headed in their direction. The light from a high-beam flashlight blinded her and she ducked her head and shivered when his evil laugh echoed through the room.

"Gotcha."

Noelle blinked and squinted, trying to see as the gunman approached. He purposefully kept the light aimed at her eyes as a way to keep her helpless. The canister of wasp spray was hidden at her side, and she knew he'd need to get close before it would be of any use. If she aimed toward the sound of his voice, she might be able to slow him down.

"Come out of there," he demanded.

She didn't move, willing him to take a few more steps. When he was so close she could smell his sweat, she brought up the canister, pointed it directly at the area where she assumed his face was located and pressed hard on the lever. He let out a yowl and brought his arm up to protect his eyes.

She jumped to her feet and made a break for the stairs, carrying Kaitlin while managing to hang on to the wasp spray. It wasn't easy to see and she hit the edge of the wall hard with her shoulder. Ignoring the pain, she forced herself to keep going. She could hear the thug swearing as he stumbled after her. She hoped he was blinded by the wasp spray since she needed every advantage she could get.

But when she reached the top of the stairs, he was already gaining on her. She darted through the kitchen, intending to head out to the backyard when he grabbed her shirt from behind and yanked her backward. In a last ditch effort, she brought up the wasp spray and shot a stream over her shoulder hoping to hit him again, but he clipped her against the side of her head and she went down, hard. At the last possible moment she turned her body so that her shoulder took the brunt of the fall as she attempted to cushion Kaitlin as much as possible. Her temple throbbed where she'd hit it on the doorframe.

She tried to scramble to her feet, still hanging on to Kaitlin, but he roughly grabbed her and yanked her upright. Kaitlin let out a scream of terror but he ignored it, pinning Noelle painfully against his massive body. When he pressed the tip of his gun against Kaitlin's head, Noelle froze, breathing heavily. Instantly, he ripped the can of wasp spray out of her hand and threw it down onto the floor with a resounding clunk.

"We're going outside and you're going to move nice and slow, understand?" he murmured harshly in her ear. "If you give me any more trouble, I'll just shoot you both here and then wait here for your boyfriend to show up. Either way, you all die. It's your choice."

She nodded as the will to fight drained out of her. There was no way on earth she would risk any harm to Kaitlin. Even though deep down she knew he'd still eventually kill them, going with him now would give them time.

Time to get away. Or time for Caleb and Declan to rescue them.

"Move," he said, giving her a nudge. She took one step and then another, grateful that the thug allowed her to keep holding Kaitlin as he half pushed, half guided her out of the kitchen and outside. The phone, squashed between her and Kaitlin, vibrated in the pocket of her sweatshirt, indicating she had a text message. She ignored it, and hoped the thug hadn't noticed. So far, he hadn't frisked her and she prayed he wouldn't think to do that now.

The intruder stayed close to her side, a hard arm clamped around her shoulders, no doubt making sure there weren't any nosy neighbors who might see the gun, as they walked across the damp grass toward another black truck parked on the street.

Noelle tried to look around to flag someone's attention, but no one was around. And within seconds, he had the back door of the extended cab open, and shoved her forward.

"Get in. And if you try to run again, I'll shoot you in the back and take the kid. A small prisoner would be easier to control anyway."

She had no intention of risking that, so she climbed into the truck, holding Kaitlin, who was now crying softly, in her lap. He held the gun ready as he quickly rounded the car and slid into the driver's seat. The minute he started the car, the automatic locks clicked into place.

"Tell her to shut up," he said harshly.

She didn't bother to acknowledge him, since there was no way to make Kaitlin stop crying. Noelle was on the verge of crying, too.

The thug drove slowly away from the curb as if they had all the time in the world. She kept her eyes trained on the rearview mirror for any sign of Caleb and Declan returning, but there was nothing but darkness behind them.

She closed her eyes and rested her cheek on the top of Kaitlin's head, trying to reassure the little girl.

Please, Lord, keep this innocent child safe in Your care. Amen.

Declan headed up the driveway and before he came to a complete stop, Caleb pushed open his car door and jumped out of the vehicle. He ran into the house through the unlocked garage door, coming to an abrupt halt when he saw the canister of wasp spray lying in the middle of the kitchen floor.

Dread seeped into his bones. "Noelle? Kaitlin?" he shouted. There was no answer. The door leading to the basement was open and the lights were on, but even as he clamored down the stairs he knew they were too late.

Noelle and Kaitlin were gone. Whoever had been inside the house had taken them.

"No," he whispered, falling to his knees on the edge of the mattress. This couldn't be happening. He and Deck had followed Brickner. So who'd taken Noelle and Kaitlin?

The accomplice, of course. Hadn't he already known that Brickner couldn't have done this without help? Not just help in getting a hold of Noelle and Kaitlin, but in setting him up for his wife's murder, the murder of Jack Owens and the murder of Kenneth James, the alleged eyewitness.

How many other people had to die? *Please, God, not Noelle and Kaitlin.*

Caleb buried his face in his hands, wishing that he could trade places with them. He'd do anything to keep them safe.

Anything.

"Caleb? Come on, buddy, you need to pull yourself together." Declan's hand was heavy on his shoulder. "Check your phone. Has she responded to your text message?"

A flicker of hope burned through the heavy veil of despair. He slowly rose to his feet and pulled the phone out of his pocket to peer at the screen. "Not yet."

"Look over here—see the spray pattern on this vent?" Declan practically dragged Caleb over to the back corner of the basement. "Smells like wasp spray, most likely from the canister upstairs. It looks like Noelle tried to fight back and escape."

He stared at the spray pattern, admiring Noelle's spunk. He forced himself to think like the cop he once was. The cop he still was, deep in his heart and soul. "I see what you mean," he admitted. "And look at the way those boxes are knocked askew. She and Kaitlin must have been hiding here. Let's go back up to the kitchen."

Upstairs, Caleb carefully examined the area, trying to visualize what had taken place. "There's a thin smear of blood here," he said, gesturing to the rust-colored stain on the oak molding around the doorframe. He fought to keep his tone steady. "Must belong to Noelle or Kaitlin since they aren't here and obviously were trying to get away."

"I see it," Declan said in a grim tone.

The thought of his daughter being hurt made his stomach cramp painfully. "We have to find them, Deck."

"We will."

He knew his buddy was trying to reassure him, to keep him from going over the edge, but as Caleb stood there, it was obvious they had no clues. Nothing to go on. No way of knowing who Brickner's accomplice might be.

"Maybe we should go back to that building where we last saw Brickner," Declan said, breaking the long silence.

Caleb brightened at that thought. "Yeah, why not? At least then we can grab him and force him to tell us where Noelle and Kaitlin are."

"Not exactly," Declan drawled. "Take a deep breath, Caleb. This isn't the time to overreact."

It was on the tip of his tongue to yell at Deck, since the guy clearly had no clue what it felt like to have your daughter and the woman you cared for in danger, but he was sidetracked by his vibrating phone. His flash of anger subsided as he grabbed the phone and quickly read the text message.

Heading north on hwy 33.

His heart leaped in his chest. "It's Noelle! We have to get in the car. She's giving us directions."

They hurried outside and jumped back in Deck's vehicle. "Highway 33 is only seven miles from here," Caleb said. "Maybe they're not that far ahead of us."

"Tell her that we're on the way," Declan said as he concentrated on driving.

He was already in the process of doing that. We're on the road, keep the info coming.

After sending the text he stared at the phone, praying for a response, even though he knew that Noelle wasn't about to take any chance of getting caught.

The fact that she was able to text him at all was a good sign. The guy who'd taken them must not have searched her, so he must not realize she had a phone. Hopefully that meant that Noelle's injury wasn't too bad. Unless the blood had come from Kaitlin? *No, don't go there.* Imaging his daughter hurt would only paralyze him.

He needed to think positive. Wasn't that what prayer was all about? To believe that God was watching over them?

"Junction Highway 33 up ahead," Declan said, breaking into his thoughts.

As much as he wanted to keep texting Noelle, he managed to refrain, unwilling to increase the possibility of getting caught. All they needed was to know her ultimate destination.

A familiar landmark caught his eye. "Deck, isn't this close to where we last saw Brickner?"

"Yeah, actually we came in from the other direction, but this is the same area." Declan didn't take his eyes off the road. "Caleb, he could be taking them to Brickner."

"Good." Caleb didn't bother to hide his satisfaction. "If that's true we should be able to blow this case wide open."

"Maybe we should call for backup," Declan said.

He glared at his buddy. "You're kidding, right? Have you forgotten there's a warrant out for my arrest? What makes you think anyone will believe me?"

"I believe you and I'm sure we could get Isaac to back us up," Deck said stubbornly. "We can't do this alone, Caleb."

Panic gripped him by the throat. Would Declan betray him now, calling for backup when they were so close?

His phone vibrated again. "'In a truck, at a four-car garage,'" he read Noelle's text out loud.

"That's the same place we saw Brickner," Declan said, pushing hard on the accelerator. "At least now we know where we're going and we should be able to get there in less than ten minutes."

Caleb texted that information back to Noelle but he didn't feel any better knowing Noelle and Kaitlin's destination. Because if Brickner was out there waiting for them, he wasn't alone. He likely had a lot of help.

He and Deck would be seriously outnumbered. Not to mention out-armed. Deck had his service weapon, but Caleb didn't have anything other than a Swiss Army knife.

Maybe Declan was right. Maybe they really did need some backup. And Isaac was a decent guy, someone he once considered a friend.

As much as he hadn't planned on trusting anyone within the sheriff's department, he couldn't deny that he'd do anything, even sacrifice his own life if necessary, to save Noelle and Kaitlin.

And if that meant he was arrested and tossed in jail for the rest of his life, then so be it.

He was about to tell Declan to go ahead and call for backup, when Deck eased on the brakes.

"I think the building is up ahead. We should probably go in on foot from here."

"I'll go," Caleb said. "There's no sense in both of us going. I'll stall until you get backup in place."

Declan looked as if he might argue, but Caleb wasn't going to sit around. He opened the car door and slid out, shutting it quietly behind him.

Declan was smart. He'd do what needed to be done.

And so would Caleb.

THIRTEEN

Noelle held Kaitlin close as the thug who'd kidnapped them drummed his fingers on the steering wheel, obviously waiting for someone to come out of the garage building to meet him. She'd managed to text Caleb a few details about where they were, but that didn't mean he'd be able to find them.

Kaitlin had stopped crying about fifteen minutes ago, after she'd soothed her fears as best she could. Noelle could only hope that the little girl was feeling a little better. She sensed the thug who'd taken them would not be happy if Kaitlin started throwing up again. Her greatest fear was that he'd do something to hurt Kaitlin, just to make her shut up.

A man came out of the building and walked toward the black truck. She thought he might be Brickner, but it was difficult to tell. The thug in the truck held his gun on her and gestured to the door. "Get out."

She swallowed hard and fumbled for the door handle while keeping a tight grip on Kaitlin. The door was heavy and she had to push it with her foot to get it open.

"Well, if it isn't Miss Whitman and O'Malley's daughter." The man's voice was low and once again she tried to get a good look at him. But he remained in the shadows. She suspected, although she couldn't see it, that he had a gun, too. "So glad you could join us."

As if they had a choice? She did her best to control the flash of anger.

There was no way to even consider making a run for it, considering the two men were armed, so she slid awkwardly to the ground, still holding Kaitlin. The truck was high off the ground and she stumbled a bit when she landed on the pavement. The child was getting heavy, but she ignored the cramping of her arm muscles.

"Take several steps forward," the man standing in the shadows commanded.

Noelle did as she was told, resisting the urge to glance around for any sign of Caleb or Declan. Even if the two men were somewhere close by, which she highly doubted, they certainly wouldn't be easily seen. She needed to figure out how to stall long enough for help to arrive.

"What do you want?" she asked as she cautiously approached the stranger. "I don't understand what's going on. Why did you bring us here?"

"I'm surprised you didn't figure it out for yourself," he said in a scathing tone. He must have been closer than she realized because suddenly he was gripping her arm hard enough to leave bruises. He forcibly dragged her toward a side door on the building. "No? Guess you're not too smart, are you? Obviously we need the kid to lure O'Malley out of hiding. You're nothing more than a glorified babysitter."

Knowing the truth should have made her feel better, but it didn't. She had no idea how she and Kaitlin could manage to escape, or if Declan and Caleb would be able to find them.

The only good thing was that the stranger, who she was now convinced was Brickner, probably wouldn't kill them yet. He'd wait until Caleb arrived. But she wished she hadn't sent Caleb the text messages. She felt certain he would give up his life for his daughter.

The only problem was that they would likely all die here. No way would Brickner let Noelle and Kaitlin go, even if Caleb did show up.

She wanted to text Caleb to let him know it was a trap, but she didn't dare do anything that would catch Brickner's attention. He roughly dragged her into the large building, which conveniently didn't appear to have any windows. There were a few lightbulbs hanging off the ceiling though, so it wasn't completely dark. In the light, she could make out the familiar face of Marc Brickner. He wasn't trying to hide his face now, so obviously he intended to kill them all.

She glanced around the building, realizing that it was smaller on the inside compared to the outside. Then she realized that there was a wall dividing the large space in half. Their half was mostly empty except for another black truck parked off to the side. She stared at the wall, wondering what was located on the other side. More men with weapons? Probably. She couldn't afford to assume there weren't others around.

"Sit over there," Brickner said, giving her a slight shove toward the farthest corner of the building.

He released her arm and she resisted the urge to rub her bruised flesh. She sat down in the corner, the concrete floor definitely uncomfortable, not that she planned to complain. When Brickner moved away she lowered her mouth to Kaitlin's ear. "How are you feeling?" she asked in a whisper. "Does your tummy still hurt?"

"A little," Kaitlin whispered back. "Can I eat a cracker?"

Noelle was surprised to realize that Kaitlin had managed to hang on to her package of crackers, although they were likely crushed into millions of small pieces after everything they'd been through. But if the crackers helped settle the child's stomach, she was all for it. "Sure," she responded.

Brickner and the thug who'd found them at Declan's house were standing together near the truck, talking in low voices. She couldn't hear what they were saying, but that didn't matter. While their attention was otherwise occupied, she risked sending another text message to Caleb.

Stay away, it's a trap.

She felt a little better after sending the message. Surely Declan wouldn't let Caleb do anything foolish. Kaitlin nibbled on a cracker while Noelle glanced around the interior of the building, searching for anything that she could potentially use as a weapon.

But there was nothing.

"I'm thirsty," Kaitlin whispered.

"I'll ask for something," she reassured the girl. Raising her voice she called out to the two men. "Excuse me, but Kaitlin's been sick, and I'd like to give her some white soda so she doesn't throw up again."

The two men swung around to face her and she shivered at the frank malice reflected in the eyes of the thug she'd sprayed with wasp killer. Even in the dim lighting she could see that his eyes were red and swollen from the harsh chemicals. If she hadn't been blinded by his flashlight, she might have actually managed to get away.

"This isn't a hotel," Brickner said with a dark scowl.

"I know, but if she gets sick, the whole place will reek like vomit," she pointed out. "Why would you want that?"

There was a long pause before Brickner turned to the guy next to him. "Ray, get the kid a soda."

Ray didn't look at all happy to be the gopher but he threw her one last look before he disappeared, she assumed, to the room on the other side of the wall.

After a few minutes Ray returned carrying a can of white soda. Brickner held his gun on her as Ray handed it to her. Up close the damage to his eyes looked even worse. "You'll pay for what you did to me," he said in his low, evil voice.

She swallowed hard, imagining the worst as she took the soda can from him, avoiding his gaze. She opened the can and held it for Kaitlin.

As thirsty as Noelle was, she decided to hold off drinking any of the soda herself. For one thing, she didn't see a bathroom anywhere. And for another, she didn't want to catch Kaitlin's bug. Besides, it was far more important for Kaitlin to remain hydrated than it was for her.

She had no illusions about how this might end up.

Kaitlin only took a few sips before pushing the can away. The little girl looked sleepy and Noelle hoped the child could manage to get some rest.

"Close your eyes. I'm right here," she said softly. "We're safe here for now."

"I love you, Noa."

Her throat closed and it took her a minute to respond. "I love you, too."

She hugged Kaitlin on her lap, running a soothing hand down the child's back, softly reassuring her that they'd be fine. Kaitlin seemed to believe her and soon the child's eyelids fluttered closed. Noelle sighed and leaned back against the coarse two-by-fours which made up the walls of the building.

Closing her eyes, she prayed.

Please, Lord, keep Kaitlin safe in Your care and Caleb, too. Amen.

Caleb forced himself to move slowly, even though adrenaline coursed through his bloodstream, making him want to run as quickly as possible. He knew Deck was calling for backup but there was no way in the world he could sit around waiting for their backup to arrive. Right now, his only thought was to find a way to convince Brickner to release Noelle and Kaitlin in order to take him instead.

The garagelike building came into view and he kept hidden among the trees and shrubs as much as possible. He racked his brain for some sort of viable plan, but so far he didn't have much. Without a weapon he couldn't even the odds in his favor. If he was captured and taken inside the building, where he was sure they were holding Noelle and Kaitlin, he might be able to use the knife. If Brickner didn't search him and find it.

Too many "ifs" for comfort.

When he was about twenty yards away, his cell phone vibrated with an incoming message. He glanced at the screen, expecting an update from Deck, but the message was from Noelle.

Stay away, it's a trap.

He stared at the message with a mixture of relief and exasperation. It was great that she was trying to warn him, but did she really think he would stay away, leaving her and his daughter to face Brickner alone?

Yeah, right. Not hardly.

I'm coming, he texted back.

With grim determination he crept closer to the building, trying to think of a way to force Brickner's hand. He wasn't armed, but Brickner didn't know that. Maybe, just maybe, he could bluff his way in.

But if that didn't work, he'd have to come up with a plan B.

Caleb waited at the corner of the building, not far from where the black truck was parked, for what seemed like forever. A glance at his watch confirmed only ten minutes had passed. Just when he was about to throw a few rocks toward the building to draw someone out, the side door opened and a tall, broad-shouldered figure came out and headed toward the black truck.

He was beginning to think that Brickner required all his goons to drive black trucks, to keep anyone from figuring out which truck Brickner might be in. Did this guy realize that he was being used as a patsy to keep Brickner's identity secret? Probably not.

Caleb waited until the guy had gotten inside the car and drove away before he made his move. There could obviously be other men inside, but there was at least one less person that he'd have to deal with. He sent Deck a quick text letting him know that the guy who'd taken Noelle and Kaitlin was leaving in the truck. With any luck, Deck and his backup team could arrest the guy and from there, they could potentially get him to squeal on Brickner.

Caleb left the corner of the building and made his way to the small group of trees that were located at a right angle to the building. When he was situated, he dug a rock from his pocket and heaved it with all his might at the garage door located on the side of the building, choosing the door closest to where the guy had just left the building. The rock hit the garage door with a resounding *crack*.

He thought he heard some activity coming from inside the building, including a few loud bangs. Then the side door opened and he saw Brickner standing there, holding a gun to Kaitlin's head.

"Come on, O'Malley, you can do better than this," Brickner taunted. "What's the matter? Are you afraid to take a shot at me for fear of accidently hitting your daughter? You never were as good of a sharpshooter as me."

Caleb had to work hard to hold his anger in check, especially because he could see that Brickner had the gun pressed tightly against Kaitlin's temple and she was sobbing soft, ragged sounds that ripped his heart to shreds. Brickner was right. Even if he had a weapon, he wouldn't use it. He'd never take a chance on hitting his daughter.

"Let her go, Brickner." He hoped his voice didn't show the depth of his fear. "Let her go and I'll take her place."

"You'll surrender now, or I'll kill her," Brickner said in a harsh tone. "Shall I count to five?"

"Are you really going to take a chance that I'll miss?" Caleb asked with a calmness he didn't feel.

Brickner hesitated, and from where he stood, Caleb could see the other man was still searching for him. "You won't sacrifice the kid. One, two, three, four..."

"Okay, okay!" Caleb stepped out from his hiding spot and put his hands up in the air. "You have me, Brickner. Now let her go."

"I'm not letting her go. Get inside the building, now."

Caleb forced himself to walk toward Brickner, keeping his hands on his head in a show of good faith that he wasn't armed. He hoped that Brickner would frisk him for a gun, without finding the knife that he'd stashed in the bottom of his shoe.

"Dad-dy," Kaitlin sobbed, her tiny face streaked with tears.

"I love you, Katydid," he said reassuringly. "Everything is going to be fine."

"Very sweet," Brickner said snidely. When Caleb was inside the building, Brickner shoved Kaitlin at him. "Here, take the kid and go sit in the corner with your woman."

Caleb gladly took Kaitlin in his arms, hugging his daughter close while praying that Deck and his backup team would get here quickly. Brickner locked the door behind him, but Caleb didn't even think of trying to rush the guy right now. First he needed to know what he was up against.

He carried Kaitlin over to where Noelle was waiting. She met him partway, giving him a desperate hug. He wrapped one arm around her, the other one still holding his daughter. For a moment he couldn't speak.

When she loosened her grip, he still didn't release her. "I'm sorry I got you into this mess," he whispered.

"It's not your fault."

Noelle was being far too kind. It was his fault, and he knew it. Maybe if he'd called Declan sooner. Maybe if he'd kept Noelle and Kaitlin in a motel instead of taking them to Declan's basement. Maybe if he hadn't gone to pick up his daughter from Noelle's house in the first place, none of this would have happened.

But it was too late to go back and change the past now. No matter how he wished he could.

"I want you to know, that if we don't make it through this for some reason, I promise we'll meet again in heaven," he told her in a quiet voice that wouldn't carry over to Brickman.

"Oh, Caleb." Noelle's eyes filled with tears. "I'm glad you believe in God, but we're not finished yet. God is still with us, watching over us."

"I know." He reached up to cup her cheek with his hand, staring intently down into her eyes. "I've been praying for you. For Kaitlin. For us."

"Me, too."

He brushed a brief kiss across her mouth, wishing there was something he could do to help Noelle and Kaitlin escape. When he lifted his head, he was certain that his regrets were reflected in his gaze. He tried to smile as he transferred Kaitlin back into Noelle's arms.

"Stay behind me," he instructed in a low voice.

She made a soft sound that he took to be a protest.

"I need to get him to talk, to stall." He didn't dare mention Declan's name, but he could see by the expression on her face that she understood what he meant.

Noelle didn't say anything more before she melted back against the wall, sliding back down to sit in the corner with Kaitlin cuddled on her lap.

Caleb turned to face Brickner—the man he knew likely killed his wife, his lawyer and his former neighbor.

What Caleb didn't know was why.

FOURTEEN

Noelle held Kaitlin close, murmuring soothing words to the child as a way to hide the depth of her overwhelming despair. She understood that Caleb was stalling, waiting for Declan to arrive in order to help get them out of here. But it seemed as if too much time had already passed by and she couldn't help thinking that Declan would be too late. Especially now that Caleb was captured and being held here, too. Brickner had exactly what he'd wanted and she feared that their time had run out.

Even Caleb's brief kiss hadn't made her feel any better because the gesture had felt too much like goodbye. She was thrilled that Caleb believed in God, and as much as she hoped they would all meet in heaven some day, that didn't mean she was ready to die just yet.

Kaitlin deserved a chance at life. Surely God would spare the child's life?

Please, Lord, save us from harm. Keep us safe in Your care. Amen.

"Why are you doing this, Marc?" Caleb asked in an overly loud voice that startled her. "I mean, I get the fact that you tried to frame me for my wife's murder, but I don't understand why you came after me once I was released from jail."

Noelle held her breath as Brickner stared at Caleb, his gun steady in his grasp.

"I found your perch in the tree across the street from Noelle Whitman's house," Caleb continued as if they were having a two-way conversation, ignoring Brickner's steely gaze. "I have to say, that was really an amazing shot."

"Don't patronize me," Brickner said harshly. "If it had been an amazing shot you'd be dead and we wouldn't be here right now."

"Pure luck on my part," Caleb said, waving away the comment and keeping his tone filled with admiration. "How could you know that I would bend down to pick up Kaitlin's giraffe at that moment? You were always a better shot than me. By far, the best sharpshooter on the team."

Noelle couldn't tear her gaze away from Brickner, searching for any sign that Caleb was getting through to him. Although she wasn't really all that hopeful, since anyone who killed the way Brickner had couldn't possibly have a heart or a soul.

"But I still don't understand why," Caleb continued as if they were old friends discussing the weather and not murder. "Why take a shot at me outside Noelle's house? Who were you going to pin that one on? I just can't quite follow your logic on that."

Brickner glanced at his watch, as if he was waiting for someone else to arrive. After a long moment he met Caleb's gaze. "I was forced to change my approach after Ken weaseled out on the original plan."

"Yeah, I figured that much. But what happened?" Caleb asked. "Why did Ken end up in Lake Michigan? Did he try to take the bribe money and run?"

"I caught him sneaking out of his house in the middle

of the night, with a one-way plane ticket in his pocket. I didn't mean to kill him, but it was his fault for getting cold feet," Brickner admitted. "If he would have testified against you, I know the jury would have sent you away for life. That stupid idiot ruined everything."

Noelle couldn't suppress a shiver at how logical Brickner made everything sound. As if he had no choice but to commit murder. To kill Ken and dump his body into the lake.

"Your plan was perfect," Caleb agreed. "Well, almost perfect."

Brickner's expression turned ugly and for a moment Noelle feared that Caleb had pushed him too far. She subtly reached up and gripped the hem of Caleb's T-shirt and gave a gentle tug, trying to warn him.

But Caleb acted as if he didn't notice. "I have to assume that you were afraid I'd start digging for the truth about Heather's death. Is that why you took a shot at me? Because you were afraid I'd figure everything out?"

Noelle tugged on Caleb's shirt harder this time. What was he thinking to keep poking at Brickner?

"Don't overestimate your importance," Brickner sneered. "I was never afraid of you."

Caleb shrugged. "Maybe you should have been. Especially since I found your secret company, Marc. Let me think, what was the name of it again? Oh yeah, Eileen's Elite Escort Services. And of course I saw Heather's photo on there."

Brickner gave a tiny jerk, making Noelle think that he hadn't expected Caleb to find out about the website. Or the escort service. But other than the small involuntary movement, Brickner didn't say anything more.

"What happened that night, Marc?" Caleb pressed.

"Why did you kill Heather? Was it because she wanted to get out of the business? Or did she break up with you?"

Noelle was practically holding her breath, waiting for his answer. She wished they had a tape recorder for the moment Brickner admitted he'd killed Caleb's wife.

"Don't be ridiculous," Brickner said in a strangled tone. Gone was his previous arrogance, instead there was a note of agony shimmering in his voice. "She didn't break up with me. I loved Heather, and she loved me, too! After she divorced you, we were going to leave and be together, forever. I would never hurt her. Never!"

Noelle felt her jaw drop and quickly closed her mouth to hide her shock. Brickner's voice practically vibrated with the truth. The hint of pain reflected in his tone seemed too real to be faked.

She could tell by how still Caleb went that he was surprised, too. And she knew exactly what he was thinking. If Brickner didn't kill Caleb's wife, then who did?

Caleb couldn't believe what he was hearing. How was it possible that Brickner wasn't the one who'd killed Heather? What on earth had happened that night?

He tried to gather his chaotic thoughts. "I'm sorry, Marc. That must have been rough on you when Heather was found shot to death." It felt odd to be talking about his wife loving another man, but deep down Caleb knew that his love for Heather had died long ago, well before she'd been murdered.

This wasn't the time to wallow in his regrets of the past. Heather was gone and he would do whatever was necessary to save Noelle and Kaitlin. He needed Brickner to confide in him. To keep talking, long enough for Deck to get here with his backup.

It was already taking far too long.

Brickner turned away, and Caleb considered rushing the guy to get Marc's weapon, but almost as soon as the thought formed, Brickner straightened and swung around to face him. "She never loved you," Brickner sneered. "Heather loved me. Only me!"

Caleb wasn't about to argue, because really what did Heather's feelings matter? She was gone and there was nothing to be gained by arguing. He'd known their marriage was over, but he'd tried to stick it out, for Kaitlin's sake.

"I believe you," Caleb said quietly. "But if you really loved Heather, why haven't you tried to seek revenge on the real murderer?"

"What makes you think I haven't?" Brickner asked. He glanced at his watch again and almost as if on cue, his cell phone rang. Brickner answered his phone, still holding the gun aimed at Caleb.

"Where have you been?" Brickner asked the caller in a terse tone. "I expected you to be here fifteen minutes ago."

There was the muffled sound of someone on the other end of the line, but no matter how hard he tried, Caleb couldn't decipher exactly what the other person was saying.

He couldn't help wondering about the identity of the person on the other end of the phone. The same person who'd killed Heather? Was this what Brickner meant when he mentioned getting revenge? Was Brickner right now setting up Heather's murderer just like he'd set up Caleb fourteen months ago? Unfortunately it seemed highly likely.

"You're not the one running this show. I am," Brickner was saying in a caustic tone. "Now you know what it feels like to be the one taking orders."

Taking orders? Caleb turned the phrase over in his mind, trying to make sense of the one-sided conversation.

Was the person on the other end of the phone someone who was normally in charge? The guy who owned Eileen's Elite Escort Services? And if so, who? A silent partner? A new player he and Declan wouldn't know or recognize?

Or could it be Sheriff Cramer? No, surely the sheriff wouldn't get involved in something like this. Sheriff Cramer didn't like him much, but the guy only had a few more years until his retirement. Why would he risk his pension at this point in his career? No, Caleb didn't buy it.

If not the sheriff, then who?

The image of Captain Will Royce flashed in his mind, and he felt a little sick at the possibility that the administrative leader of the SWAT team was a far more likely candidate to be involved in Brickner's scheme. Royce sometimes filled in on the SWAT team, so he certainly knew the guys. And Royce fancied himself to be a ladies' man, too. Was it possible he was the co-owner of the escort service?

Or worse, had Royce killed Heather in a fit of anger?

"I don't like a last minute change of plans," Brickner was saying. "We go with the original plan or I'll just kill them all here and let you deal with the mess."

Caleb didn't like the sound of that. Obviously their time was running out. Whoever the guy was on the other end of the line, he certainly wasn't doing Caleb and Noelle any favors.

"Glad you agree," Brickner said smugly. "You have ten minutes to get here, understand?"

Caleb tried to consider the proposed ten minutes to

be a positive sign. At least Brickner wasn't going to start shooting yet.

As long as the caller showed up, that is.

There was no way to know for sure, but if the caller was Royce then Brickner's comments made sense in a sick sort of way. For some reason, Brickner had something to hold over the caller to make him do whatever Brickner wanted.

A cold chill snaked down his spine. If Royce really was involved, he hoped and prayed that Declan wouldn't tip off the captain when arranging for backup.

Because if Royce got a whiff of Declan's rescue plan, then they were certainly doomed to die tonight.

Noelle glanced up as Caleb took a step backward, turning his head and talking in a voice so soft she could barely hear. "Text D," he whispered. "Tell him to stay away from Royce."

Noelle nodded and eased her hand back into the pocket of her sweatshirt, where she still had her phone hidden. She had no idea how much battery life she had left, and prayed that there would be enough for the text to go through.

Texting without watching what she was doing wasn't easy. She typed the message and then tried to glimpse at what she'd written to make sure it was right. Using Kaitlin's body to help shield the light, she peered at the screen.

The message was a bit mangled so she quickly fixed it and then pushed the send button. There was only one bar of battery left, but she didn't turn off the phone. She intended to give Declan the chance to track them here through the phone, if at all possible.

Where was Declan? Why wasn't he here already?

"Noa, my tummy hurts," Kaitlin whimpered.

Up until now, the child had been relatively quiet, her hysterical sobs had faded once Brickner had given her back to Caleb. Noelle was very worried that the little girl would start screaming at any moment from her night terrors, especially at the way Brickner kept putting the gun to her temple as a way to force them to do what he wanted. Noelle had almost forgotten about the flu bug.

"What's wrong?" Caleb asked.

"She feels sick to her stomach," Noelle murmured. "Here, Kaitlin, try another sip of the white soda."

Kaitlin obediently sat up and took the can between her palms and sipped from the opening. "Can I have another cracker?"

"Sure." Noelle picked up the horribly crumpled package of crackers and tried to find a piece amid the crumbs. She pulled out a half cracker and gave it to Kaitlin. "Try this, see if it helps your tummy."

"Listen, Marc, my daughter has the flu," Caleb said. "Why don't you let her go? You have me. You don't need her."

"Nobody goes anywhere until I tell you to," Brickner said firmly. "Don't worry, the flu bug isn't going to be bothering your daughter for long."

Noelle swallowed hard, knowing exactly what Brickner was insinuating.

"Kill me if you want, but let my daughter go. She's five years old, hardly a threat to you or anyone else."

"She's not a threat, but she is a part of my master plan," Brickner corrected. He glanced again at his watch and Noelle could almost see his frustration. "If he's not here in five minutes…" Brickner's voice trailed off.

"Then what?" Caleb challenged. "Then you're going

to kill us all here? And what story will you leak to the press? Who will you blame for our murders?"

The faint sound of an engine broke the silence and Brickner smiled grimly. "He's lucky he made it in time."

"In time for what?" Caleb asked, and Noelle could hear the desperation in his tone.

"You'll find out soon enough," Brickner said.

There was a knock on the door, must have been some sort of prearranged code, two short knocks, then a pause, and then two more knocks again. Brickner took several steps backward in order to unlock and open the door.

Caleb tensed as the stranger walked into the room, also armed with a gun. Noelle struggled to her feet, still carrying Kaitlin, wanting to be ready for anything.

"I figured you'd show up sooner or later, Royce," Caleb said to the newcomer. "I knew Brickner wasn't smart enough to do all this on his own."

Noelle gasped when Brickner pulled the trigger on the gun. A shot rang out at the exact same moment Caleb hit the floor.

"Silence!" Brickner roared. "Or I'll shoot again and this time I won't miss!"

Noelle was shaking so badly she feared she'd drop Kaitlin, but Caleb came up to a low crouch and after a few minutes she realized he wasn't bleeding.

Caleb hadn't been hit.

But now, the odds of their ability to escape seemed even more impossible.

Caleb took several deep breaths, realizing he'd pushed Brickner just a bit too hard.

But where was Declan? Why hadn't Deck stopped Royce from coming inside?

"Is everything set?" Brickner asked Royce, as if the

shooting incident hadn't happened. He was beginning to wonder if Brickner had some sort of psychological disorder the way he ran hot and cold in a matter of minutes.

"Yes. Everything is ready," Royce said, looking as if he were scared to death of Brickner. How had the captain gotten involved in all of this?

"Good." Brickner gestured at Caleb with his gun. "All three of you, get in the truck."

The black extended cab truck was parked over to the south side of the building. Caleb didn't move, knowing that once they got inside the truck, their chances of getting away dropped considerably.

"Why?" he asked. "Where are you taking us?"

The expression on Brickner's face reflected evil. "We're going back to where this all started. Now get inside, or I'll shoot you in the kneecap."

Caleb glanced back at Noelle and Kaitlin, his expression full of regret. "Let's go," he said softly.

Noelle looked as if she might collapse, but she moved toward the truck with surprising strength. He would have taken over carrying Kaitlin, but he wanted to have his hands free, just in case. He still had the knife in his shoe. Maybe when Royce was driving he could use it to help them escape.

"Move!" Brickner thundered, his patience obviously wearing thin.

Noelle instinctively picked up the pace, and he followed close behind, protecting her as best he could. He almost wished that Royce would end up being assigned as their driver, because he was fairly certain that Brickner had completely lost his marbles somewhere along the way.

Caleb took Kaitlin long enough for Noelle to scramble into the backseat. He gently set his daughter beside

Noelle and then took the seat beside her, so that Kaitlin was safely tucked in between the two adults.

Caleb closed the truck door and then quickly reached into his shoe for the knife. It was only a small pocket-knife but it was better than nothing.

To his dismay, both Royce and Brickner climbed into the front seats. Royce was the designated driver and Brickner sat at an angle where he could easily keep his weapon pointed at Noelle.

Royce twisted the key, bringing the engine to life with a loud roar. He pushed a button on the dash and the garage door opened. Royce drove out of the building, and hit the button again to close the overhead garage door behind them.

Caleb tried not to search for signs of Declan, because he didn't want to tip off either Royce or Brickner that help was on the way. Or so he hoped.

"Give up, O'Malley," Brickner said. "There's no one here to help you."

Caleb froze. Had he somehow given something away to Brickner?

"We took care of your friend Declan Shaw," Brickner said with a smile that didn't reach his eyes. "The three of you are on your own."

Caleb licked his dry lips, hoping, praying that Brickner was bluffing. Brickner knew that Noelle and Kaitlin were hiding at Declan's house. Brickner must have assumed that Declan had been with Caleb at some point.

Surely Deck was too smart to get caught in Brickner's trap. Caleb wanted, desperately, to believe Brickner was just playing mind games with him.

"Sit back, relax. We have a good fifteen-minute ride before we reach our destination," Brickner said.

"And where exactly is that?" Caleb forced himself to ask. "Where did this all start?"

Brickner laughed, but it was not a pleasant sound. "Your house, O'Malley. This all started at your house. And that's exactly where it's going to end."

FIFTEEN

Noelle struggled to keep calm, but she was shaking so badly she feared the men in the front seat could actually feel the seat move. She was losing hope that Declan would be able to save them. And with two armed men now, instead of just one, she didn't know how she and Caleb could save themselves.

She wished now that they'd made their move while they were in the garage with just Brickner there. Surely the odds had been better then?

But it was too late to go back now. Noelle had been praying nonstop since this nightmare began and she'd continue until she took her last breath. The way things were looking now, she was praying that death would come quickly and without undue suffering.

Especially for Kaitlin. She closed her eyes against the burn of tears. Facing her own death was one thing, but she couldn't bear to think of the little girl dying tonight.

"Why did you kill Jack Owens?" Caleb asked as the big black truck ate up the miles.

"He was a loose end," Brickner admitted. "Once we found you, we didn't need him anymore."

Noelle wished Caleb would stop asking questions, because the more she heard the greater the fear that clawed at her belly. These men were not going to let them live. What was the point of knowing exactly what had transpired earlier? What difference did any of that make now?

"Who botched the car explosion?" Caleb asked.

Royce's hands tightened on the steering wheel in a way that convinced Noelle that he was the one who'd set the bomb. She was tempted to cover her ears so she couldn't hear any more, but realized that asking questions like this must be Caleb's way of dealing with stress. To keep them talking.

Maybe even to distract them.

She took a deep breath and did her best to swallow the hard lump of fear choking her. She needed to stay strong. For Kaitlin's sake.

"Another mistake," Brickner said tersely. "But there will be no more, isn't that right, Royce? You're going to get the job done this time, aren't you?"

"Yes, sir," Royce muttered.

An incredulous expression filtered across Caleb's face and she knew that seeing his former boss like this, bowing down to Brickner's authority, must be strange. The interaction between the two men wasn't at all reassuring. Clearly, Royce was going to do whatever Brickner told him to do as the guy calling the shots. Why, she had no idea.

"You see, Caleb, once we're finished here tonight, everyone will believe that all three of you died in a murder/suicide," Brickner said in a matter-of-fact tone.

"Yeah, right. No one who knows me will believe that," Caleb said. "Everyone knows my daughter is my life."

"Oh, trust me, they will believe exactly what we want them to. We've planted enough evidence to make it look as if you and the preschool teacher were having a hot affair even prior to Heather's murder. And of course, she threatened to take your daughter away from you, so you had no choice but to kill them both before you tragically took your own life."

Noelle couldn't bear to hear any more. The way Brickner talked she knew that he'd indeed have planted enough evidence to make the authorities and the media buy their story. And why not, when he'd had the captain of the SWAT team to add credence to his lie? She didn't know why Royce was involved, and at this moment, she didn't care.

She glanced out the passenger-side window, but it was too dark to see much and what little she could make out didn't look at all familiar. Even if she had the chance to run away with Kaitlin, she wasn't sure where to go to find safety.

The truck slowed as Royce turned into a ritzy subdivision. The houses weren't packed close together the way they were in Declan's neighborhood. She was shocked at seeing the high-end lifestyle Caleb once enjoyed. She found it hard to imagine what his life must have been like during the years he was married to Heather.

Although looking at him now, with a grim expression etched on his face, she knew he'd give up everything he owned in a heartbeat if it meant keeping them safe. The knowledge made her feel a little better. Caleb was a different man now than what he'd been before.

"Almost home," Brickner said with fake cheerfulness.

Caleb reached over to take her hand, giving it a reassuring squeeze. The resolute expression on his face caused her stomach to knot, painfully. This was it. Now that they'd reached their final destination, she was certain that Caleb would make one last attempt to save them.

Or die trying.

She shook her head, trying to tell him without words

not to do anything foolish. But he only nodded, reaffirming her fears while subtly pointing to the small space on the floor behind the driver.

She could tell exactly what he wanted her to do. Get Kaitlin down and out of the line of fire so that he could make his move on Brickner. She gave a small nod to indicate she understood.

Royce turned the truck into a long, curved driveway in front of a large redbrick house with white trim and black shutters. Caleb's house was located at the end of a cul-de-sac, tucked between several trees, a good hundred feet away from the road. It was surprisingly isolated and her hopes of being rescued plummeted even further.

This was it. Noelle put her arm around Kaitlin while keeping her gaze focused on Brickner. She had to assume that Caleb would do something drastic during the time they were about to get out of the vehicle, especially the minute Brickner's gun was no longer pointed directly at her, Noelle knew she had to do what was needed to protect Kaitlin. The child must survive no matter what happened.

This is it, Lord. We are putting our lives and our fate in Your hands. May Your will be done. Amen.

Caleb gripped his small penknife in his right hand, waiting for the exact moment to make his move. Brickner was seated directly in front him, but he didn't dare attempt to stab the guy while Marc's gun was pointed at Noelle.

Timing was critical. The second Brickner moved to get out of the vehicle he'd have to move his gun enough that Noelle wouldn't be in the line of fire. That was the moment he needed to strike. He silently prayed for forgiveness for what he was about to do.

Dear God, forgive me for my sins and give me strength to save Noelle and Kaitlin.

"Okay, we're going to get out of the car, nice and easy," Brickner instructed. "The woman and the kid go first."

Caleb could see the stark fear reflected in Noelle's eyes and wished he could reassure her. He tried to let her know that the plan was still to get down, and truthfully if Noelle and Kaitlin could safely get out of the truck they'd have a better chance at surviving if they could somehow crawl underneath the massive frame.

Noelle's gaze clung to his for a long moment as she moved slowly and deliberately, opening her passenger door and then sliding out until her feet were planted on the ground. She reached for Kaitlin and his daughter went willingly into Noelle's arms. Noelle bent down to set Kaitlin on her feet and the way she had her head bent toward the child, as if peering down at the ground, Caleb could tell that Noelle had already figured out that she needed to get Kaitlin hidden beneath the truck.

"Whoops, did you fall, Kaitlin?" Noelle asked, bending over Kaitlin as if she were helping the child when in fact she was practically shoving his daughter to her knees.

The minute Noelle was ducked down and Kaitlin was safely out of sight, Caleb reached up and stabbed Brickner in the neck with his small penknife, hoping to disable the guy rather than trying to kill him.

"Argh!" Brickner cried out in pain, and Caleb jerked at the sharp retort of Brickner's gun.

"Get down!" Caleb shouted, reassured when Noelle dropped down out of sight.

Another muffled gunshot echoed through the night, and Caleb ducked, trying to figure out who was shooting.

It was too dark to see much. Did Brickner have backup planted here for an ambush? Had Caleb stepped from one bad situation into a second, more deadly one?

But then he saw Marc Brickner crumpled on the concrete driveway, blood soaking through his white shirt beneath his fancy suit.

Caleb stared at his former teammate in shock. Who'd taken the shot at Brickner?

"Royce," Brickner whispered.

Caleb frowned and leaned closer. "What did you say?"

Royce was still in the driver's seat of the truck. Was Brickner trying to tell him that Royce shot him?

"Make him pay. Royce…killed her. Killed…Heather." Brickner stared at Caleb as if willing him to believe. "Make him pay."

"Why?" Caleb asked.

"He…wanted her…for himself…" Brickner managed. He coughed and then his eyelids fluttered closed.

"Marc?" Caleb reached out to check Brickner's pulse, but he already knew. His former teammate was dead.

Caleb didn't know if he should believe Brickner, although remembering how the guy professed to love Heather, he was inclined to go along with his theory. Besides, it made sense that Brickner had something to hold over Royce's head, to get the captain to do his bidding.

What better motive than to threaten to go to the police with the truth about Heather's murder?

Another gunshot echoed through the night and Caleb ducked down when he heard the shattering of glass. He instinctively glanced up, but the window in the car door above his head was still intact.

"Don't shoot! I give up! I give up!" Royce shouted in a panicked tone as he climbed out from behind the wheel. "Do you hear me? I give up!"

"Toss down your weapon!" a familiar voice shouted from a cluster of trees. "Now!"

Declan?

Caleb lifted his head in time to see Royce toss his weapon halfway down the driveway and then lift both his hands in the air in the universal gesture of surrender.

Almost instantly, three of Caleb's former SWAT team members emerged from behind the trees on either side of the driveway. One guy swooped on Royce's gun, safely taking possession of the weapon. A guy who looked like Isaac Morrison grabbed Royce and turned him around so that he faced the hood of the truck, pulling Royce's hands behind his back in order to cuff him. He tensed, wondering if he was the next one to be arrested but Deck crossed over and slapped him on the back.

"Nice work," Declan said. "Stabbing Brickner like that was exactly what Isaac needed to get the guy in position to make his shot."

"I can't believe you're here," Caleb said, feeling as if he were in a daze. "How did you know we were coming to my place? Why didn't you meet us out at the garage?"

"It's a long story," Declan admitted. "We managed to convince Royce to cooperate. In turn, Royce fed Brickner information that I was captured, too. I think Royce sensed his time with Brickner was coming to an end. He told us he believed Brickner was going to kill him."

"Really? You convinced Royce to turn against Brickner?" Caleb shook his head. "I'm shocked."

"We'll have plenty of time to fill you in on the details, later." Declan glanced down at Brickner. "Is he dead?"

"I think so." Caleb couldn't drum up any sympathy for the man who'd killed so many. And in that moment, he didn't care about what had happened. Deck was right. They were finally safe and that's all that mattered.

"Noelle?" Caleb called. "It's safe for you and Kaitlin to come out now."

"Hey, Caleb?" Isaac called as he finished the job of cuffing their former boss. "You better get over here. I think she's bleeding."

"What?" Caleb frantically pushed past Declan and rounded the truck, where his heart nearly stopped in his chest when he saw Noelle's body sprawled facedown on the driveway. He dropped to his knees and reached for her, desperately trying to feel for her pulse. "Noelle? Are you all right? Can you hear me?"

Kaitlin was lying mostly beneath the truck, and when she saw him she began to cry. "Daddy, help Noa. Please help Noa!"

"I will, sweetheart. Come on out now, you're safe." He reached out a hand to his daughter, silently urging her to come out from beneath the truck. "The bad guys are gone now. We're all safe."

"Noa," Kaitlin sobbed. She crawled forward and grabbed Noelle's hand, giving it a hard shake. "Wake up, Noa. Wake up!"

In the background Caleb could hear Declan calling for an ambulance. He closed his eyes and concentrated, thankful to feel the faint flutter of Noelle's pulse. Relieved to know she was still alive, he gently turned Noelle over to try and find the source of the bleeding.

"Isaac, get me some light!" he said urgently.

Isaac pulled out his flashlight and aimed down on Noelle, who looked far too pale as she lay unconscious on the driveway.

"Don't die, Noelle," Caleb muttered half under his breath. "Please don't die."

"She's hit just beneath her shoulder," Isaac said, shining the light on the area. "Looks like the entry wound is on the front and the exit wound is in the back. You'll have to hold pressure on both sides to stop the bleeding."

Caleb was already stripping off his shirt. "Come on, Noelle, hang in there. You're going to be all right. Don't give up on us, do you hear me? Don't give up!"

He placed his balled-up shirt beneath her right shoulder, using the weight of her body to help put pressure on the bleeding. "Give me your shirt," he said to Isaac.

Isaac stripped off his shirt and passed it over to Caleb. "She'll be okay, Caleb. It's just a shoulder wound."

Caleb nodded, not bothering to argue that she could die of a shoulder injury if her lung was hit. He could barely tear his gaze from Noelle, even as he leaned on her shoulder wound to help stop the bleeding. She was an innocent bystander in all of this. A mess he'd dragged her into without giving her a choice.

He couldn't bear to lose her.

Not when he hadn't gotten a chance to tell her how much he loved her.

The wail of sirens filled the air, telling him that help was on the way.

"Please, Lord, keep Noelle safe in Your care. Please heal her wounds and spare her life," he whispered.

"Amen," Kaitlin responded in a tearful voice.

He was humbled by his daughter's ability to pray. Thanks to Noelle's teaching, his daughter knew more about faith and God than he did.

He was so thankful, not only for this second chance at having a future with his daughter, but for discovering faith and God. He owed Noelle so much more than he could ever repay.

When the ambulance pulled up and the paramedics jumped out, hurrying over with their medical gear, he reluctantly eased back so they could begin working on

SIXTEEN

Engulfed in a shroud of pain, Noelle gradually became aware of her surroundings. The sharp scent of antiseptic along with the beeping sounds of a monitor confirmed she was in the hospital and her heart squeezed with fear. Her entire body hurt from the beatings. She tried to open her eyes to make sure her foster father wasn't anywhere around. What if he came to finish what he'd started? What if he made good on his threat to silence her forever?

"No," she forced the word through her parched throat, blinking her eyes to get rid of the blurred vision.

"Just relax, Noelle." The deep male voice came from somewhere near her left shoulder.

She jerked away, turning as far as she could over onto her right side, cowering against the side rail while she desperately searched for the call light. Where were the nurses? Didn't they understand Frank was the one who put her here in the first place? Why had they left her alone with this monster?

"Noelle, what's wrong? Are you in pain? Should I call the nurse?"

She felt a heavy hand on her shoulder and she flinched, trying to get even farther away from the threat. *No! Help me! Please, Lord, help me!*

"You must be in pain, I'm getting the nurse. Try not to move around so much, you might pull out your stitches."

She'd already found her call light and had pushed the button frantically, hiding her hands amid the folds of the blanket covering her. When the heavy hand moved from her shoulder, she forced herself to turn her head to face the threat. Her vision swam, then sharpened, and she frowned when she realized that the man standing beside her wasn't Frank Petrol, her foster father.

It took another minute for her to recognize the stranger as Caleb O'Malley. She blinked again and tried to gather her scattered thoughts. "What happened?" she whispered in confusion. "Are we safe?"

Caleb's dark eyes were full of concern. "Yes, we're safe. But unfortunately you took a bullet in your left shoulder. Can you feel the padded dressing there? You just came out of surgery a few hours ago. The doctor said you'll be fine, even though you'll need to have a lot of physical therapy to get your full range of motion back."

Now that he mentioned it, the pain in her shoulder became almost unbearable, radiating down her arm and ricocheting through her back. Obviously rolling over in bed hadn't been the smartest move. She slowly eased onto her back and tried to take some slow, deep breaths to calm her racing heart.

She'd never had a flashback like this before, probably because she hadn't been a patient in a hospital since the initial incident ten years ago. But the memory had been horrifyingly real. In that moment she thought for sure she was the sixteen year old who'd been beaten with a cane, her foster father's favorite tool for doling out punishment. The coppery taste of fear still tasted bitter on her tongue and she shied away from the painful memories.

"The nurse should be here shortly," Caleb murmured. He stood a good foot from the side of her bed with his hands tucked into the front pockets of his jeans and it dawned on her that he thought she'd been afraid of him. And she had, but only when she'd thought he was Frank.

"I'm sorry," she whispered again through a throat that felt like it was on fire. "Water?"

"Good morning," a perky blond-haired nurse greeted them as she entered the room. "My name is Jennifer and I'll be your nurse for today. How are you feeling?"

"Hurts," Noelle admitted.

"I've brought you some pain medication, but first I need you to rate your pain on a scale from zero to ten, with ten being the worst pain you've ever felt in your entire life and zero being pain free." As she spoke Jennifer pulled up a laptop computer on wheels and logged in.

"Ten," Noelle said, wondering just how many patients actually gave a zero after having surgery. Was this some sort of torture test to make the patients wait for their pain medication?

"Can she have a sip of water, too?" Caleb asked.

"Sure, let me give her pain meds first." Jennifer used some sort of gadget to bar-code her wristband and then the medication, hitting more keys on the computer before she actually got to the point of inserting the syringe of pain medication into her IV port.

Noelle avoided Caleb's gaze as Jennifer helped her sit forward enough to take a sip of water. She was deeply appalled at how she'd responded when she first woke up. She couldn't imagine what Caleb had thought of her reaction. Even now, she could feel his curious gaze penetrating deep, as if he were willing her to tell him what happened.

Something she'd rather avoid if possible.

She'd thought she'd gotten over her past. But apparently she'd only buried it. Now she knew exactly what Kaitlin's night terrors were like for the little girl.

The coolness of the ice water slipping down her sore throat felt wonderful. She eased back against the pillows and glanced around. "Where's Kaitlin?"

"Sleeping right here behind me." Caleb took a step sideways so she could see the little girl curled in the seat of the recliner, Caleb's sweatshirt covering her like a blanket. "She's been out for several hours now. Not surprising, after all the excitement from last night."

"She's okay?" she asked, desperate for reassurance. "She wasn't hurt?"

"She's fine, mostly worried about you," Caleb admitted, his brown eyes intense. "She prayed for you, too. You've taught her well, Noelle."

Tears pricked Noelle's eyes at the thought of the precious little girl praying for her safety. The pain Noelle felt in her shoulder was well worth the outcome.

"I'm glad she's safe," Noelle murmured. "I was so scared for her."

"Do you need anything else?" Jennifer asked, in her annoyingly perky tone.

"No, I'm fine." Thankfully the pain medication had already taken the edge off, making the pain tolerable. Gingerly, she shifted in her bed, trying to get comfortable.

A strained silence hung suspended between them the moment the nurse left. She wished Caleb would leave and take Kaitlin home so the child could sleep in her own bed. There was nothing more he could do here.

"Brickner's dead?" she asked, breaking the silence.

"Yeah and Royce is under arrest. Declan and Isaac saved the day. And just before Brickner died, he claimed Royce was the one who killed Heather."

She swallowed hard and nodded. She vaguely remembered the sound of gunfire just before the burning pain that had sent her to her knees. Before she lost consciousness she heard Royce giving himself up.

"Will the police finally believe you?" she asked.

"I think so, especially now that I have Deck and Isaac to back me up."

"Good." She was sincerely happy for him. All Caleb wanted was to clear his name and find out who really killed his wife.

"Noelle, are you sure you're okay?" he asked in a low voice. "You looked scared to death when you woke up."

She closed her eyes for a moment, wishing she could avoid this conversation. But it was too late to hide her reaction, and maybe Caleb deserved to know the truth.

The sooner he knew, the sooner he'd leave her alone. Their time together was over. He was finally free to live his own life and she would go back to being a preschool teacher. Their nightmare was over.

So why did she want to cry?

"Noelle? Please, talk to me. I'm worried about you."

She couldn't ignore his plea, no matter how much she wanted to. Baring her soul would be difficult but if that was what he needed before he left once and for all, then she'd tell him.

"I…was in the hospital once before, about ten years

ago," she admitted. "When I woke up, I thought I was sixteen again."

"What happened back then?" he pressed, gently. "Why were you so afraid?"

Caleb reached over to take her hand, but Noelle couldn't bear to look him in the eye. "When I heard your voice, I thought you were my foster father, Frank. He used to…hurt me."

"What? He sexually assaulted you?" Caleb asked hoarsely, his hand tightening on hers.

"No, he only beat me with a cane."

"That's bad enough, Noelle. I hope they arrested him and tossed him in jail."

She bit her bottom lip and shook her head. "I didn't hang around long enough to find out. I ran away, and lived on the street for a few weeks."

"Oh, Noelle," he murmured, brushing a strand of hair away from her cheek. Thankfully she didn't flinch again at his touch and she hoped the flashback was safely in the past where it belonged.

She shrugged her good shoulder. "Don't feel sorry for me. I was lucky to end up in a homeless shelter, where I found a wonderful woman by the name of Abby Carrington. Abby took me under her wing, taught me about faith and God, helped me get a job as a waitress and finish my GED. I even managed to get a small scholarship into college. So you see? I was one of the lucky ones."

"I admire you so much, Noelle," Caleb murmured. "After everything you've been through, you still found a way to believe in me, believe in my innocence. And then you did whatever was necessary to protect my daughter. I owe you so much. I don't know how I'll ever be able to repay you."

"Just take good care of Kaitlin," she said, trying to

fight off the sedative effects of the narcotic. Her mind was getting foggier by the minute. "That's all I ask. Goodbye, Caleb."

She thought she heard Caleb say her name before she succumbed to sleep.

Goodbye? Caleb stared down at Noelle's peaceful features, resisting the urge to shake her awake. What did she mean goodbye? Was this it? Was this her way of saying she didn't want to see him anymore?

He sank down onto one of the uncomfortable plastic chairs in the corner of Noelle's hospital room and scrubbed his hands over his face. He tried to push back the wave of panic. Surely Noelle hadn't really meant to tell him goodbye. That must have been the narcotics talking.

He couldn't bear the thought of not having Noelle in his life. Yet he couldn't deny that she may not feel the same way. She hadn't pushed him away when he'd kissed her, but maybe now she was having second thoughts.

He rubbed his palms into his eye sockets trying to erase the image of Noelle flinching from his touch, cowering in her bed. The thought of someone beating her with a cane filled him with a helpless fury. What kind of foster parent would do that? Why hadn't anyone stood up for her? She'd been a child, and children were meant to be protected. Not abused.

He was lucky that Kaitlin had ended up with Noelle as a foster mother. The idea of his daughter being subjected to the same abuse that Noelle had suffered made him sick to his stomach. His thoughts drifted back to the first time they'd met, when Noelle had hugged Kaitlin and Kaitlin had shied away from him. Noelle's past had likely made her more determined to protect Kaitlin, even from him.

And he didn't blame Noelle one bit for being leery of him. In fact, knowing what he did now, he was amazed Noelle had managed to trust him at all.

"Caleb?"

He lifted his head to find Deck hovering in the doorway. "Yeah?"

"It's time for you to give your statement."

He grimaced and nodded. "Who's leading the investigation? Sheriff Cramer?"

"Internal Affairs has taken over the investigation," Declan confided. "Sheriff Cramer is on the hot seat at the moment. IAB is all over him. He has some explaining to do since Royce reported directly to him and, of course, Brickner was dirty, as well. I doubt Cramer will make it through unscathed, even if he didn't know about Brickner's and Royce's involvement with Eileen's Elite Escort Services. Cramer will never get reelected after this."

Caleb hadn't been overly fond of Sheriff Cramer, but that didn't mean he wanted to see the guy lose his job. Back when he'd been locked up in jail, he'd have been happy to get revenge, but now, he was simply glad to be alive and reunited with his daughter.

And even more grateful to have found Noelle and God.

"Lieutenant Erickson is waiting for you in a small conference room down the hall," Declan advised.

"Can you stay here with Kaitlin for a while?" Caleb asked, rising to his feet. "I don't want to wake her up just yet."

"No problem." Deck crossed over and took the chair Caleb had just vacated.

Caleb glanced over his shoulder at Noelle one last time before he slipped from the room.

He found the conference room without any trouble and when he saw Lieutenant Erickson sitting there in his full dress uniform, Caleb paused and took a deep breath, hoping and praying he wasn't about to be arrested again.

Surely Deck would have warned him if there was any possibility of that. Wouldn't he?

"Come in, O'Malley," Lieutenant Erickson said, rising to his feet.

Caleb forced himself to step forward, taking Erickson's outstretched hand. "Lieutenant."

"Have a seat." Erickson waved him toward the empty chair located perpendicular to his. Erickson glanced down at his fat file folder for a moment before meeting Caleb's gaze. "I'm here to listen to your side of the story and I need for you to start at the beginning."

Caleb stared at the senior officer for a moment. "You mean the night of my wife's murder? Or just since I've been released from jail?"

"We have your statement from the night your wife was murdered," Erickson said, tapping the folder with his pen. Caleb understood he wasn't about to get an apology for what had transpired. "And from what your former teammates said, it appears you really were innocent of that crime. But I want to know exactly what transpired since the moment you left the jail with your lawyer, Jack Owens."

Caleb took it as a good sign that the lieutenant at least appeared willing to listen. He began his story, telling how Jack had taken him to run a few errands, including stopping at the bank and picking up a new cell phone, before dropping him off at home. Caleb described how he'd narrowly missed getting shot when he'd gone to pick up his daughter and how he'd convinced Noelle to go with him to escape the gunman.

"Why didn't you call the police?" the lieutenant demanded.

"With all due respect, sir, I didn't trust anyone, but I especially didn't trust the police."

Erickson grunted as if he couldn't think of a good argument to refute his statement. "Okay, so then what?"

Caleb described how they'd found a motel with a pool and that he'd exchanged license plates and then had talked to Owens late at night. He explained that they'd stayed longer the next day, to allow Kaitlin time to swim, which is how they managed to avoid being killed when the vehicle exploded.

Lieutenant Erickson was taking notes fast and furious while Caleb talked. "You escaped on foot?" he asked incredulously.

"Yes, sir." Caleb described their journey back to Madison on the chartered bus. He described how he'd searched on the internet to find the SWAT member Noelle had seen the night of Heather's murder, and how she'd recognized Marc Brickner.

"We'll get to Brickner and Royce in a moment," Erickson said. "What happened after Madison?"

"We took a bus to Milwaukee and headed over to meet with Jack Owens. But he was dead inside his condo."

"And yet you still didn't call the police?" Erickson asked with a deep scowl.

"No, sir. By then we already knew that the body of Kenneth James had been found in Lake Michigan and that I was a suspect for his murder. I knew that Jack's death would be pinned on me, as well. And I was right.

After I contacted my buddy Declan Shaw, I discovered there was a warrant out for my arrest." It wasn't easy to keep the accusation from his tone. The more he talked about everything that happened, the more his resentment grew. Why hadn't anyone realized that he was being set up? Why hadn't anyone given him the benefit of the doubt?

"All right, then what happened?" Erickson asked.

He shook his head. "I don't know the details. You'll have to ask Noelle Whitman once she's recovered from being shot, but Brickner had someone kidnap Noelle and my daughter, Kaitlin. We were following Brickner and it was pure luck that we saw Noelle and Kaitlin being taken inside the garage where we'd found Brickner. We never did find out what was on the other side of the building. From that point on we were focused on getting Noelle and Kaitlin out of there alive."

"So you saw Brickner holding them hostage?" Erickson asked.

"Yes. He held his gun at my daughter's head, forcing me to give myself up." The memory was enough to make him break out into a cold sweat. "He spoke to Royce on the phone and then the two of them took us at gunpoint over to my house. Brickner told me the plan was to make my death along with Noelle's and Kaitlin's deaths look like a murder/suicide."

Erickson's mouth tightened with anger. "Did he confess to killing your wife, too?"

"No, sir. He admitted that he killed Kenneth James, because the guy was trying to skip town with the money he was paid to be an eyewitness against me. Brickner also admitted that he arranged for Jack's murder, so that he could pin everything on me." Caleb let out a heavy sigh. "But as he lay dying on my driveway, he told me to make Royce pay for killing Heather."

At this point, Erickson tossed his pen down and sat back in his chair. "That doesn't mesh with Royce's side of the story."

A chill snaked down Caleb's spine. He leaned forward, knowing he needed to make Erickson believe him. "Listen, Lieutenant, Brickner was a sociopath and deserved to die. But I believe he really loved Heather. He told me they were planning to get married after our divorce was finalized. I can't think of one good reason he'd kill Heather."

Erickson crossed his beefy arms over his rotund abdomen. "You said it yourself. He was a sociopath. He probably killed her and then tried to put the blame on Royce."

Caleb couldn't believe what he was hearing. They were going to let Royce walk! They were feeling bad for the guy, no doubt believing whatever sob-story Royce fed them.

"But why would Brickner admit to the other murders but not to killing Heather?" he pressed. "I think he would have taken the credit if he had in fact done the crime."

"Could be that he was just trying to get back at you, make you feel bad about his affair with your wife," Erickson pointed out.

"Listen to me. The man was dying. He told me to make sure Royce paid for murdering Heather. Why would Marc make up a story when he was about to die?"

"Did anyone else hear him say that?" Erickson asked.

Caleb thought back, trying to remember. "Deck was there less than a minute later. He may have heard it."

Erickson glanced down at his notes. "Nope, he didn't. Okay, that's all for now, O'Malley. I'll get in touch if I have any other questions."

Caleb stared at the lieutenant for several heartbeats,

wrestling with his temper. He bit his tongue and forced himself to leave the room without losing control.

He slowly walked back to Noelle's room, grappling with the fact that Royce was actually going to get away with murder.

And there was absolutely nothing he could do about it.

SEVENTEEN

Noelle woke up several times throughout the day, and each time there was no sign of Caleb or his daughter. Jennifer, her nurse, claimed they left about an hour before lunch. Noelle told herself that it was better this way, but that didn't ease the ache in her heart.

By late afternoon the nurses and therapists made her get up out of bed to walk the halls. The pain radiating from her shoulder was still bad, but somehow the physical pain didn't mean much in the wake of her emotional turmoil.

She shouldn't be surprised that Caleb had left with his daughter, after all she was the one who told him goodbye. So what if Caleb had kissed her? It wasn't like a mere kiss meant anything these days. They'd been running for their lives while trying to figure out who'd killed Caleb's wife and set him up for her murder. They were forced to spend time together, and that closeness had heightened their emotions. She knew very well that under normal circumstances a man like Caleb wouldn't look at her twice. After all, he hadn't recognized her as one of the preschool teachers who cared for his daughter.

Frank had been a firefighter, physically fit, the macho type of guy who secretly used his fists on his wife and a cane on his foster child. She felt a little ashamed at how she'd thought Caleb might be like Frank. Caleb had never said much when he came to pick up Kaitlin, and he'd always looked gruff and impatient as if he had far better things to do.

Not that he'd ever been short with Kaitlin. In fact, his daughter had always raced over to throw herself into her father's arms.

But that was before he'd gone to jail for a crime he didn't commit.

She learned more about who Caleb really was during their brief time together. She knew she could trust Caleb not to hurt her physically. She'd never once seen him lose his temper or lash out at anyone. Frank used to hit the wall or the table when he was mad, and from there it wasn't long until he'd started hitting people.

No, in that respect Caleb would never hurt her or his daughter. But could she trust a man like Caleb with her heart? Through the time they'd spent together, she'd grown to care for him. Maybe, even had fallen in love with him. But what did she know about real love? She'd never had a serious relationship, always shying away from men. The very thought of opening herself up to rejection made her break out into a cold sweat.

She couldn't help thinking about Caleb though as she worked on the simple exercises the therapist left for her to do on her own. She suffered through a brief interrogation by Lieutenant Erickson, who wanted to know all the details about what had happened since Caleb had showed up on her doorstep that fateful Friday afternoon. She assumed that he'd spoken to Caleb, too, which explained his absence.

But she'd thought for sure Caleb would return to visit

with Kaitlin after dinner, but the hours crept by slowly with no sign of them.

By eight o'clock in the evening, when there was an overhead announcement about the end of visiting hours, she knew they weren't coming. Disappointment slashed deep. It had obviously been the right choice to keep her feelings to herself. Caleb was already moving on with his life and honestly, she couldn't blame him. He'd already spent fourteen long months behind bars.

He deserved every moment of freedom. And she'd known all along that once this was over he wouldn't need her anymore.

She squeezed her eyes tight to keep from crying but a few tears leaked out and slid down her cheeks. So she did the only thing she could, she prayed.

Help me to move on with my life, too, Lord. Please guide me along Your path. Amen.

Caleb spent the afternoon with Kaitlin, Declan and Isaac at his house, once the crime scene from the driveway had been cleared. He played with his daughter, but then put in a Disney movie for her so that he could strategize with his former teammates.

"There has to be some proof we can find to nail Royce for Heather's murder," Caleb said in a low tone.

"Not easy since it seems like the only one who knew the truth is dead," Deck muttered with a scowl.

"I think Cramer is going to offer you your old job back," Isaac said. "He's already down two men and I think he wants to try and salvage his image."

"His image is beyond repair," Deck scoffed. "But giving Caleb his job back is the least Cramer could do. Caleb could easily sue the department for defamation of character and false imprisonment."

Caleb sighed. "Come on, you two, focus. While it would be great to get my job back, if we can't figure out a way to link Royce to Heather's murder he'll be a free man in less than ten years. All they have against him right now is being a party to the crime. And considering he's claiming Brickner threatened his life if he didn't cooperate, they'll likely go easy on him."

"You have to admit, Brickner could have been lying," Isaac pointed out.

"He wasn't." Caleb was positive Marc was telling the truth. "Why would he bother? And besides, there had to be something big that Brickner was hanging over Royce's head in order to make him cooperate. Why not Heather's murder? Maybe Brickner walked in on him shortly after Royce killed her and the two of them trumped up this scheme to set me up in order to keep Heather's involvement in the escort service a secret."

"You're right, but we'd have to prove Royce was having an affair with your wife," Deck said thoughtfully. Then he grimaced. "Sorry, Caleb."

Caleb flashed a wry grin. "I've already seen her photograph on that sleazy website. There's nothing more that would shock me."

"Daddy, *Shrek 1* is over. It's time for *Shrek 2!*" Kaitlin shouted from the other room. She ran into the kitchen and climbed up onto Caleb's lap. "When can we see Noa?" she asked.

He forced a smile. "She's still groggy from her surgery, remember? We'll go tomorrow, when she's feeling better, okay?"

"Okay. I'm hungry. Can I have a snack?"

At times like this he wished Noelle was here to guide him. Was Kaitlin supposed to have snacks in the late afternoon? Wouldn't that ruin her dinner? But then again, she slept in this morning after being up half the night, and she was recovering from the flu, so maybe a snack was a good idea?

Why didn't kids come with an instruction manual?

"Ah, sure, Katydid. What would you like?" he asked.

"Fish crackers and juice," she announced.

That sounded like something Noelle would give her so he set Kaitlin down and pulled out the crackers and filled a glass with juice. He let her take her snack into the living room, even though he knew Noelle would not approve. But he didn't want to talk about murder within earshot of his daughter.

"Try not to spill, okay?" he said.

"Okay."

When he walked back into the kitchen, Deck and Isaac were deep in a low conversation. A conversation that halted abruptly the moment he entered the room.

"What's up?" he asked when the two of them stared at him.

Deck and Isaac exchanged a long look before Deck cleared his throat. "Caleb, don't get mad, okay? But we think you should have a paternity test done on Kaitlin."

Anger flashed hard and swift. "Get out," he bit off between clenched teeth.

"Caleb, we're only trying to help," Declan began but he cut him off quickly.

"No. Get out," he repeated. "I'm not kidding. I'm not going to listen to your garbage for another minute."

His two teammates exchanged a tense look before they slowly rose to their feet and made their way to the door.

"Caleb, she'll always be your daughter. No one can take her away from you. But if there's a chance that her DNA matches Royce's…"

Caleb slammed the door, cutting Declan off midsen-

tence. He paced the short length of the kitchen, wishing
he could hit the gym to let off some steam.

"Daddy, I spilled," Kaitlin cried out from the living
room.

He grabbed a dish towel and hurried into the other
room, knowing that he only had himself to blame for
the cherry stain on his carpet.

The mess was the least of his worries. He did his best
to ignore Declan and Isaac's suggestion, but he found
himself searching Kaitlin's features for any resemblance
to him.

Kaitlin had her mother's glossy blond hair and her
big blue eyes. Surely Kaitlin had his nose, and his chin.
No, wait, she had a cleft chin and he didn't. Although
neither did Heather.

But Royce did.

No, he wasn't going to do it. Cleft chins likely skipped
a generation, that's all. He'd never met Heather's parents,
but he'd bet her father had a cleft chin.

He wanted to smack Declan and Isaac for planting
the seeds of doubt in his mind. He tried to concentrate
on the movie, but after about twenty minutes he went to
find the old family photo albums. He scoured the faces
of Heather's parents and his own.

And the sick feeling in his gut told him the guys could
be right. That there was a possibility he was not Kaitlin's
biological father.

He closed his eyes and prayed for strength to do what
was right. *Guide me, Lord. Should I really do this? I
just don't know. Please help me do the right thing, Lord.
Amen.*

Noelle was woken up at the ridiculous time of five-
thirty in the morning to have her labs drawn and her vi-

tals taken. Thankfully she fell asleep for another hour and a half, before she woke up to the grumbling of her stomach.

"You have bowel sounds," Jennifer said in an approving tone, as if this was some great trick. "Good job! That means you can order full liquids for breakfast."

"Yippee," Noelle said weakly. How pathetic was she, that the thought of drinking her breakfast actually sounded good?

"I'll call for your tray. It should be here in less than an hour. And the doctor wants to switch you to oral pain medication today. So I brought two Percocets for you."

Accustomed to the routine, she gave her pain score as a seven, and waited for them to be scanned before she swallowed the meds. She knew they'd make her walk around and do her exercises so skipping the pain pills wasn't an option.

The trauma surgeon came in about an hour later with his team of residents. She stoically braced herself as they took down the dressing and peered intently at her incision.

"No signs of infection," Dr. Lauder said with satisfaction. "We'll keep you here on IV antibiotics for another thirty-six hours and by then you'll be ready to go home."

"Great," she said with a strained smile. "Can't wait."

"Do you have someone at home that can help you?" Dr. Lauder asked as one of his underlings redressed her wound.

Her smile faded. "No, but I'll manage." She refused to even consider calling Caleb.

"Hmm, we'll have the social worker come in to set up some home health visits, then," Dr. Lauder informed her. "Any other questions?"

"No questions," she confirmed, wondering if she

could somehow ask the nurse to tell the social worker she wasn't interested. The social worker assigned to her case as a child in the foster system hadn't been the least bit helpful and in fact, had refused to believe the stories of Frank's abuse.

She wasn't interested in talking to another one. She'd rather struggle along on her own.

The physical therapists kept her busy for a few hours and by the time they were finished, her shoulder felt like it weighed ten tons. She'd just returned to bed when there was a knock at her door. For a moment she was tempted to feign sleep, but then realized she wasn't a kid anymore. She could tell the social worker to leave if she wanted to.

"Come in," she called, steeling herself to be polite but firm.

"Noa!" Kaitlin cried, running into the room. "I've missed you!"

"Oh, Kaitlin, I'm so glad to see you, too!" She couldn't hide the surge of joy that engulfed her. Maybe Caleb had only come back for his daughter's sake, but right now, she didn't care. Kaitlin tried to climb onto the bed, but Caleb stopped her.

"Noelle still has a big owwie on her shoulder," he said. "You can't hurt her, okay?"

"Okay, I'm sorry, Noa."

"It's all right, Kaitlin. Here, let me give you a little hug, okay?"

She managed to hug Kaitlin with her right arm and to gently kiss the top of the little girl's head. She noticed that today Caleb had dressed his daughter in neon-pink, one of her favorite colors.

"How are you feeling, Noelle?" he asked, his gaze full of concern.

"Much better," she said. "I'm sore now, but that's because I just finished therapy."

"You look better," he said as he pulled up a chair next to her bed.

"Daddy, I'm going to color Noa a picture, okay?"

Noelle noticed that Caleb had come prepared with a coloring book and box of crayons to help keep Kaitlin busy. He was obviously doing a great job of being a single dad.

She was happy for him, and tried not to feel sad for herself.

"Noelle, I need your advice on something," Caleb said quietly. His voice was so soft, she sensed he didn't want his daughter to overhear.

"What's wrong?"

"Nothing's wrong," he assured her. "I don't know if you heard that Marc Brickner claimed that Royce killed Heather before he died."

She nodded. "Yes, I gave my statement to Lieutenant Erickson and he asked if I'd overheard Marc saying anything that night."

"Did you?" His gaze was full of hope.

"I'm sorry Caleb but I didn't hear him. I was on the other side of the vehicle. I remember trying to protect Kaitlin and then getting hit by the bullet, nothing more."

"I know." Caleb stared at his hands for a minute. "I already knew that Heather had an affair with Brickner, but according to Marc, Royce had also been with her and he flew into a jealous rage and killed her."

"I'm sorry, Caleb," she said, reaching out to take his hand. "I'm sorry you had to go through all this."

A faint smile tugged at the corner of his mouth. "We've both had difficult situations to get through, haven't we? As tough as it's been, I'm still very thankful for everything I have."

Her heart swelled with love and she had to bite her tongue to stop herself from blurting out her feelings.

"Noelle, Deck and Isaac suggested I get a paternity test done on Kaitlin. To see if there's any chance that Royce might be her blood father."

Her jaw dropped open, and she quickly glanced over to make sure Kaitlin wasn't paying attention to the conversation. "Are you going to do it?" she asked.

"I don't know what to do," he confessed, his gaze full of agony. "I love my daughter. She's the center of my life, regardless who fathered her."

"I know you love her, and she loves you, too." Her heart was breaking for him and she thought that if Declan walked through the door right now she might be tempted to throw something at him, like her box of tissues or her cup of ice chips. Why had he put the idea in Caleb's head? "There's no reason to torture yourself over this, Caleb. She's yours and that's all that matters."

He nodded, but then shrugged. "I never noticed it before, but Kaitlin really doesn't look like me. And she has a cleft chin, just like Royce. I searched through all the family photo albums last night, not a cleft chin to be seen on anyone else."

She didn't want to admit that she'd noticed the lack of resemblance, too. "Do you really think that this test will help prove Royce's guilt?"

"I think it's the best shot we have," he replied. "As much as I detested Marc Brickner, I believe he really loved Heather. And he wanted me to know the truth because he wanted to make Royce pay for what he did."

"Sounds like you've talked yourself into it," she murmured.

"Yeah, maybe. It will take a while for the DNA to get back, regardless."

"Are you sure all this hasn't changed your feelings for Kaitlin?" she asked.

"I'm positive." This time, his smile reached his eyes. "I love her. And I want you to know, Noelle, that I care about you, too."

She blinked, wondering if she'd imagined that last part. "I care about you, too, Caleb," she said carefully. "We've been through a lot together over the past week."

He cradled her hand between his. "Noelle, I don't want to scare you, or to rush you, but I want you to know, that my feelings for you aren't going to fade away over time. I missed you terribly and we were apart for less than twenty-four hours. Staying away so that you could get the rest you needed was almost impossible. I can't tell you how many times I walked to the door, intending to head over here to see you. And it didn't help that Kaitlin asked about you, constantly."

She stared at him in shock. Was she dreaming? *If so, please don't let her wake up.*

"Noelle, I know you're sick and in pain, but I just want to know that you'll give us a chance. After you feel better, of course. But don't shut me out. Don't hide from me. I love you, Noelle."

"Oh, Caleb," she whispered, her eyes brimming with tears. "I want more than anything to be with you, but I'm also afraid. I've never been in a serious relationship before. And you know I have a lot of baggage."

"I do, too," he reminded her. "And I'll be patient, as long as you give me a chance. I'll wait as long as you need."

She was honored and humbled by his declaration. "Caleb, how did I get so lucky to meet you? I never knew what it meant to be in love until I met you."

"Lucky?" he asked in mock horror. "I'm pretty sure it's the other way around. I'm the one who's lucky enough to have found you."

"God gets the credit for bringing us together," she said firmly.

"You're right. And it's up to us to honor His gift." Caleb rose and leaned over to give her a gentle kiss. She reached up to hug him with her good arm, longing for the day she could hug him properly.

"Daddy! Are you kissing Noa?" Kaitlin's voice made Caleb jump back and Noelle stifled a giggle as she glanced over to see Kaitlin gawking at them, holding a purple crayon in her tiny fist.

"Yes, I'm definitely kissing Noa," he said. To prove his point, he kissed Noelle again before he turned to face his daughter. "Are you okay with that, Katydid?"

"Oh yes, because I love Noa, too."

Noelle smiled through her tears, knowing she was truly blessed to be surrounded with love.

EPILOGUE

Six months later...

Caleb stood at the front of the church, waiting for his two favorite women to make their appearance. The church was crowded with the parishioners they'd come to know and his SWAT team buddies, including Declan standing beside him as his best man. He'd been reinstated on the force with a new boss at the helm and things were going about as well as could be expected, considering the reputation of the team had taken a serious media hit.

Caleb resisted the urge to tug at the tight collar of his tux, because he'd wear anything, including this monkey suit, if it made Noelle happy.

He was the luckiest man in the world to have this second chance at a family. Royce had crumpled after discovering he was Kaitlin's biological father, but since his former captain was serving a life sentence for his crimes, Caleb could afford to feel a little sorry for the guy.

The music swelled and everyone stood, rose to their feet and turned expectantly toward the back of the church. Kaitlin walked down the aisle first, adorably serious as she took slow steps, deliberately dropping pink rose petals on the white runner.

When her tiny basket was empty she smiled at him

and came over to stand next to him. He put his arm around her slim shoulders and said, "Good job, Katydid."

"I love you, Daddy," she whispered back.

Noelle's friend and maid of honor, Sarah Germaine, came down the aisle next with Declan. When Deck came over to stand beside Caleb, he patted the pocket holding their rings and winked.

Caleb practically held his breath waiting for Noelle. When she walked toward him, their gazes clung and instantly the crowd of people in the church faded away, leaving just the two of them.

Noelle was so beautiful, smiling confidently as she approached. When they first met, in those terrified hours after the shooting, she reminded him of a frightened gazelle determined to protect his daughter. But once the danger was over and they had a chance to relax and get to know each other, Noelle's strength and confidence had grown. The way she smiled and laughed convinced him she was truly happy.

He hoped the love he felt was evident in his eyes, the way her love glowed from hers. And he couldn't stop himself from taking a step forward to meet her.

"You're so beautiful, Noelle," he whispered. "I love you so much."

"I love you, too, Caleb," she whispered back with a quick smile.

His heart swelled in his chest as he tucked her hand in his arm and they turned together to face the pastor. With Noelle on one side and his daughter on the other, he was more than ready to begin the next phase of his life.

Noelle and Kaitlin were his family. And he would never take his life and his freedom for granted ever again.

* * * * *

Dear Reader,

Welcome to my new miniseries SWAT: Top Cops! Living in Wisconsin I've had the unfortunate experience of two terrible mass shooting incidents in the past few years. The first was the Sikh Temple Shooting and the second was the Azana Salon Shooting. In both cases, we were lucky to have an awesome response from our Milwaukee County and Waukesha County SWAT teams. Seeing these brave men and women in action as these tragedies unraveled gave me the idea to write a miniseries about them.

Wrongly Accused is the first book in the series. Caleb O'Malley has been arrested for killing his wife. When he's released from jail, he's determined to pick up his daughter, Kaitlin, and to figure out a way to start their life over. But when the bullets fly, Caleb has no choice but to take Kaitlin and her foster mother, Noelle Whitman, with him to keep them safe. Soon, Noelle's love and faith helps Caleb to learn to trust again.

I hope you enjoy reading Caleb and Noelle's story. I'm always thrilled and honored to hear from my readers and I can be reached through my website at www.laurascottbooks.com, on Facebook at Laura Scott Author and on Twitter @laurascottbooks.

Yours in faith,
Laura Scott

Questions For Discussion

1. In the beginning of the story, Caleb resents the fact that Noelle has been taking care of his daughter while he was in jail for a crime he didn't commit. Discuss a time when you resented someone else, even if that person was doing something good.

2. Noelle isn't sure she can trust Caleb, even though she knows that we should consider people innocent until proven guilty. Discuss a time when you didn't give someone the benefit of the doubt.

3. Caleb discovers how Noelle has been teaching Kaitlin to pray, despite the fact that he wasn't a Christian. Do you think Noelle did the right thing in teaching Kaitlin to pray? Why or why not?

4. Noelle soon begins to believe in Caleb's innocence because he goes out of his way to make his daughter happy and seems determined to keep her safe. Do you think Noelle trusted Caleb too soon? Why or why not?

5. Caleb is thankful that his daughter learns to trust him again. Discuss a time in your life when you experienced a strained relationship with someone you loved.

6. Caleb begins to pray when they are on the bus and the police have arrived at the mall to search for them. Discuss a difficult time in your life when you turned to prayer.

7. Noelle is determined to help Caleb prove his innocence and to find his way to God. Discuss a time when you had to help someone in your life find faith or rebuild their reputation.

8. Caleb finally calls on his former SWAT teammate Declan for assistance. Do you think he should have called his teammates sooner? Why or why not?

9. Caleb learns the true meaning of prayer when he discovers Noelle and Kaitlin have been taken from Declan's house. He's also willing to give up his life for his daughter's. Discuss a time when you might have faced a similar situation.

10. Toward the end of the story, Caleb discovers he may not be Kaitlin's biological father. Discuss whether or not you could handle learning that sort of information and how it might affect your love for your child.

COMING NEXT MONTH FROM
Love Inspired® Suspense

Available May 6, 2014

FAMILY IN HIDING
Witness Protection • by Valerie Hansen
Exposing a black market baby ring has cost Dylan McIntyre everything. Reuniting with his estranged wife and children in witness protection is the only way to keep them safe. But has he led the criminals he hoped to escape to his family's doorstep?

BODYGUARD REUNION
Guardians, Inc. • by Margaret Daley
A stalker is on the loose, and Chloe Howard plans on stopping him. But this means working closely with former flame T.J. Davenport. Can they rekindle their trust in each other before time runs out?

TRAIL OF SECRETS
The Cold Case Files • by Sandra Robbins
Ambushed by gunmen, Callie Lattimer's life hinges on cracking open a cold case. But as she and Detective Seth Dawtry uncover answers, they discover the real threat is closer than they ever thought possible....

GRAVE DANGER • by Katy Lee
The discovery of skeletal remains catapults sheriff Wesley Grant into the most dangerous case of his career. Now his only hope of catching a murderer is the beautiful forensic anthropologist who thinks *he's* the killer!

DOUBLE AGENT • by Lisa Phillips
CIA Agent Sabine Laduca will stop at nothing to find her brother's killer, but having to depend on Delta Force Major Doug Richardson to stay alive is the last thing she wants.

TREASURE POINT SECRETS • by Sarah Varland
When treasure hunters killed Shiloh Evans's cousin, she dedicated herself to finding justice. But her police training doesn't prepare her for a new series of attacks—beginning on the same day her ex-fiancé arrives in town.

LISCNM0414

REQUEST YOUR FREE BOOKS!
2 FREE RIVETING INSPIRATIONAL NOVELS
PLUS 2 FREE MYSTERY GIFTS

YES! Please send me 2 FREE Love Inspired® Suspense novels and my 2 FREE mystery gifts (gifts are worth about $10). After receiving them, if I don't wish to receive any more books, I can return the shipping statement marked "cancel." If I don't cancel, I will receive 4 brand-new novels every month and be billed just $4.74 per book in the U.S. or $5.24 per book in Canada. That's a savings of at least 21% off the cover price. It's quite a bargain! Shipping and handling is just 50¢ per book in the U.S. and 75¢ per book in Canada.* I understand that accepting the 2 free books and gifts places me under no obligation to buy anything. I can always return a shipment and cancel at any time. Even if I never buy another book, the two free books and gifts are mine to keep forever.

123/323 IDN F5AC

Name	(PLEASE PRINT)

Address	Apt. #

City	State/Prov.	Zip/Postal Code

Signature (if under 18, a parent or guardian must sign)

Mail to the **Harlequin®** Reader Service:
IN U.S.A.: P.O. Box 1867, Buffalo, NY 14240-1867
IN CANADA: P.O. Box 609, Fort Erie, Ontario L2A 5X3

**Are you a current subscriber to Love Inspired Suspense books
and want to receive the larger-print edition?
Call 1-800-873-8635 or visit www.ReaderService.com.**

* Terms and prices subject to change without notice. Prices do not include applicable taxes. Sales tax applicable in N.Y. Canadian residents will be charged applicable taxes. Offer not valid in Quebec. This offer is limited to one order per household. Not valid for current subscribers to Love Inspired Suspense books. All orders subject to credit approval. Credit or debit balances in a customer's account(s) may be offset by any other outstanding balance owed by or to the customer. Please allow 4 to 6 weeks for delivery. Offer available while quantities last.

Your Privacy—The Harlequin® Reader Service is committed to protecting your privacy. Our Privacy Policy is available online at www.ReaderService.com or upon request from the Harlequin Reader Service.
We make a portion of our mailing list available to reputable third parties that offer products we believe may interest you. If you prefer that we not exchange your name with third parties, or if you wish to clarify or modify your communication preferences, please visit us at www.ReaderService.com/consumerchoice or write to us at Harlequin Reader Service Preference Service, P.O. Box 9062, Buffalo, NY 14269. Include your complete name and address.

LIS13R

SPECIAL EXCERPT FROM

Love Inspired.
SUSPENSE

*Can an estranged couple find a way to mend fences when
they're forced into Witness Protection together?*

*Read on for a preview of FAMILY IN HIDING
by Valerie Hansen, part of the WITNESS PROTECTION
series from Love Inspired Suspense.*

Grace parked in the shade across from the school and released her three-year-old from his booster seat and looked
for her two children.

It wasn't hard to spot her eldest. His red hair stood out
like a lit traffic flare at an accident scene when he left the
main building and started in her direction. Then he paused,
pivoted and ran right up to a total stranger.

The man crouched to embrace the boy, setting Grace's
nerves on edge and causing her to react immediately.

"Hey! What do you think you're doing?"

The figure stood in response to her challenge. The brim
of a cap and dark glasses masked his eyes, yet there was
something very familiar about the way he moved.

Grace gaped. It couldn't be. But it was. "Dylan?"

He placed a finger against his lips. "Shush. Not here. We
need to talk."

When he removed the glasses, Grace was startled to
glimpse an unusual gleam in her estranged husband's eyes,
as if he might be holding back tears—which, of course, was
out of the question, knowing him.

"If you want to speak to me you can do it through my
lawyer, the way we agreed."

"This has nothing to do with our divorce. It's much more important than that."

Grace's first reaction was disappointment, followed rapidly by resentment. "What can possibly be more important than our marriage and the future of our children?"

"I'm beginning to realize that my priorities need adjustment, but that's not why we have to talk. In private."

"What could you possibly have to say to me that can't be said right here?"

"Let me put it this way, Grace," Dylan said quietly, cupping her elbow and leaning closer. "You can either come with me and listen to what I have to say, or get ready to save a bunch of money, because you won't have to pay your divorce attorney."

"Why on earth not?"

Dylan scanned the crowd and clenched his jaw before he said, "Because you'll probably be a widow."

*Will Grace and Dylan find a way to save
their marriage and their lives?
Pick up FAMILY IN HIDING to find out.
Available May 2014 wherever
Love Inspired® Suspense books are sold.*

SPECIAL EXCERPT FROM

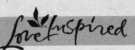

Widowed mom Suzie Kent is desperate to help her troubled son. Is her only hope the man she blames for her husband's death?

Read on for a preview of
HER UNLIKELY COWBOY by Debra Clopton,
Book #3 in the SUNRISE RANCH series.

"Suzie Kent. It's good to see you." Tucker McDermott's eyes crinkled around the edges, but concern stamped his expression, as if he knew the dismay shooting through her.

Her breath had flown from her lungs and she had no words as she looked into the face of the man she held responsible for her husband's death.

The man she was also counting on to help her save her son.

The man she wasn't prepared to see, though she'd just driven three hours with a moving van and plans to live on Sunrise Ranch, the ranch his family owned and operated.

Her world tilted as she realized whose clean, tangy aftershave was teasing her senses and whose unbelievably intense gaze had her insides suddenly rioting. His hair was jet-black and his skin deeply tanned, making his deep blue eyes startling in their intensity.

"Tucker," she managed, hoping her voice didn't wobble.

Moving to Dew Drop, Texas, to Tucker's family's Sunrise Ranch, asking for his help, had taken everything she had left emotionally—and that hadn't been much, since her husband had given his life in the line of duty for fellow marine Tucker two years earlier.

LIEXP0414

Tucker grimaced, trying to keep most of his weight off Suzie and Abe, but his hip clearly hurt.

"Thank y'all for helping me," he said, his gaze snagging on hers again and holding. "I've got it from here, though." He pulled one arm from around her and the other from around her son, Abe.

"Are you sure?" she asked, even though she wanted to step away from him in the worst way. "Do we need to get you to your vehicle?

Tucker limped a few painful steps away from them. "I'm okay," he said gruffly. "It'll just take a few minutes for the throbbing to go away." He glanced ruefully at the donkeys on the road. "What a mess. They act like they own the road."

Abe chuckled. "They sure took you out."

"By the way, I'm Tucker McDermott. I was a friend of your dad's and I owe him my life. He was an amazing man." Tucker cleared his throat. "I'm glad you've come to Dew Drop. And the boys of Sunrise Ranch are looking forward to meeting you."

Will this cowboy heal her family—and her heart?

Pick up HER UNLIKELY COWBOY to find out.
Available May 2014
wherever Love Inspired® Books are sold.